The Passion According to G. H.

CLARICE LISPECTOR was a Brazilian novelist and short story writer. Her innovation in fiction brought her international renown. References to her literary work pervade the music and literature of Brazil and Latin America. She was born in the Ukraine in 1920, but in the aftermath of World War I and the Russian Civil War, the family fled to Romania and eventually sailed to Brazil. She published her first novel, *Near to the Wildheart* in 1943 when she was just twenty-three, and the next year was awarded the Graça Aranha Prize for the best first novel. Many felt she had given Brazillian literature a unique voice in the larger context of Portuguese literature. After living variously in Italy, the UK, Switzerland and the US, in 1959, Lispector returned with her children to Brazil where she wrote her most influential novels including *The Passion According to G.H.* She died in 1977, shortly after the publication of her final novel, *The Hour of the Star*.

CLARICE LISPECTOR

The Passion According
to G. H.
(A paixão segundo G. H.)

Translated from the Portuguese, with a note, by Idra Novey
Introduction by Caetano Veloso
Edited by Benjamin Moser

PENGUIN BOOKS

PENGUIN CLASSICS

Published by the Penguin Group

Penguin Books Ltd, 80 Strand, London WC2R ORL, England

Penguin Group (USA) Inc., 375 Hudson Street, New York, New York 10014, USA

Penguin Group (Canada), 90 Eglinton Avenue East, Suite 700, Toronto, Ontario,
Canada M4P 2Y3 (a division of Pearson Penguin Canada Inc.)

Penguin Ireland, 25 St Stephen's Green, Dublin 2, Ireland (a division of Penguin Books Ltd)

Penguin Group (Australia), 707 Collins Street, Melbourne, Victoria 3008, Australia
(a division of Pearson Australia Group Pty Ltd)

Penguin Books India Pvt Ltd, 11 Community Centre, Panchsheel Park,
New Delhi – 110 017, India

Penguin Group (NZ), 67 Apollo Drive, Rosedale, Auckland 0632, New Zealand
(a division of Pearson New Zealand Ltd)

Penguin Books (South Africa) (Pty) Ltd, Block D, Rosebank Office Park,
181 Jan Smuts Avenue, Parktown North, Gauteng 2193, South Africa

Penguin Books Ltd, Registered Offices: 80 Strand, London WC2R ORL, England

www.penguin.com

Originally published as *A paixão segundo G. H..* Published by arrangement with the
Heirs of Clarice Lispector and Agencia Literaria Carmen Balcells, Barcelona.
First published in the United States of America by New Directions Publishing
Corporation 2012
Published in Penguin Classics 2014
003

978-0-141-19735-7

www.greenpenguin.co.uk

Penguin Books is committed to a sustainable
future for our business, our readers and our planet.
This book is made from Forest Stewardship
Council™ certified paper.

Contents

Introduction

I READ *THE PASSION ACCORDING TO G. H.* AS SOON AS the book came out, in 1964. I was in my early twenties. Clarice had been an illumination when I was seventeen. The story "The Imitation of the Rose," which I read in a magazine, had fascinated and frightened me. My older brother started buying all of her previously published books for me. I discovered in her other stories the same thing I had seen in "The Imitation of the Rose": a language that transformed itself in order to allow an event to emerge with the power of an epiphany, amidst the humdrum concerns of a normal life (usually a woman's life).

That transformation of language created a kind of lyrical prose that I had never before encountered. That lyricization erased the text—which nonetheless is always a narrative, never a poem—in order to allow some nearly unspeakable thing to appear. The thing.

In "The Imitation of the Rose," a woman, after a successful psychiatric treatment, goes mad once again at the sight of a bunch of roses. Daily happiness, so harshly reconquered, cannot resist the direct experience of something like an impersonal

God, and the experience makes her housewifely existence impossible.

All the other stories I read of Clarice's at that time had the same basic power, and pointed in the same direction. Their elegance made them perfect objects: each was a dangerous adventure, a miracle of composition. While reading them, the aesthetic experience itself spurred me to think about the experience of being. When I read *The Apple in the Dark*, it seemed to me that the novel was not ideally suited to Clarice's inspiration (I still hadn't read *Near to the Wild Heart*).

But *The Passion According to G. H.* remade—and radicalized—her most beautiful stories. Unlike them, however, it itself wasn't beautiful. Or maybe it was even more beautiful—but that beauty was hard for me to perceive. In the middle of the book, the narrator says that she had never before had so little fear of bad taste. She had written "billows of muteness" to refer to the content that forced her to use words like a life raft, clinging to them in order to float atop the muteness that fell upon her in successive waves. She would never before have used that expression because she respected "beauty and its intrinsic moderation."

Well, I missed that moderation, which made her short stories read like perfect songs. But I had already been ensnared by the immoderate reflexive disorder of this new beginning of Clarice's. Here, the characteristics of two extreme and perhaps non-narrative texts come together. These are among the finest texts she produced: the dirge for the murdered gangster Mineirinho, in which her observations on the yawning divisions of Brazilian society emerge so pungently, and the interminable and labyrinthine meditations on "The Egg and the Hen."

And then *G. H.* appears as a novel above and beyond perfection. It's not a story that leads the reader to philosophical thoughts. And it's not a philosophical treatise that needs a story to convey them. Instead, it is a vivifying experience that leads a person to the most ambitious philosophical discoveries. An experience transformed into literary art, in which harmony and disorder are the price of the revelation.

A younger friend said, back in the Bahia of my early twenties: "I don't like it much: it's pantheism." We were crazy kids. Now I think that this novel of Clarice's (for me the most beautiful of them all) tells us more about the possibility that Spinoza wrote his *Ethics* in Portuguese than about the dispute between immanentists and transcendentalists.

CAETANO VELOSO

To Possible Readers

This book is like any other book. But I would be happy if it were only read by people whose souls are already formed. Those who know that the approach, of whatever it may be, happens gradually and painstakingly—even passing through the opposite of what it approaches. They who, only they, will slowly come to understand that this book takes nothing from no one. To me, for example, the character G. H. gave bit by bit a difficult joy; but it is called joy.

C. L.

"A complete life may be one ending in so full identification with the non-self that there is no self to die."

—Bernard Berenson

The Passion According to G. H.

———————— I'M SEARCHING, I'M SEARCHING. I'M
trying to understand. Trying to give what I've lived to somebody else and I don't know to whom, but I don't want to keep
what I lived. I don't know what to do with what I lived, I'm
afraid of that profound disorder. I don't trust what happened
to me. Did something happen to me that I, because I didn't
know how to live it, lived as something else? That's what I'd
like to call disorganization, and I'd have the confidence to venture on, because I would know where to return afterward: to
the previous organization. I'd rather call it disorganization because I don't want to confirm myself in what I lived—in the
confirmation of me I would lose the world as I had it, and I
know I don't have the fortitude for another.

If I confirm my self and consider myself truthful, I'll be lost
because I won't know where to inlay my new way of being—if
I go ahead with my fragmentary visions, the whole world will
have to be transformed in order for me to fit within it.

I lost something that was essential to me, and that no longer
is. I no longer need it, as if I'd lost a third leg that up till then

made it impossible for me to walk but that turned me into a stable tripod. I lost that third leg. And I went back to being a person I never was. I went back to having something I never had: just two legs. I know I can only walk with two legs. But I feel the useless absence of that third leg and it scares me, it was the leg that made me something findable by myself, and without even having to look for myself.

Am I disorganized because I lost something I didn't need? In this new cowardice of mine—cowardice is the newest thing to happen to me, it's my greatest adventure, this cowardice of mine is a field so wide that only the great courage leads me to accept it—in my new cowardice, which is like waking one morning in a foreigner's house, I don't know if I'll have the courage just to go. It's hard to get lost. It's so hard that I'll probably quickly figure out some way to find myself, even if finding myself is once again my vital lie. Until now finding myself was already having an idea of a person and fitting myself into it: I'd incarnate myself into this organized person, and didn't even feel the great effort of construction that is living. The idea I had of what a person is came from my third leg, the one that pinned me to the ground. But, and now? will I be freer?

No. I know I'm still not feeling freely, that once again I'm thinking because I have the objective of finding—and for safety's sake I'll call finding the moment I discover a way out. Why don't I have the courage just to discover a way in? Oh, I know I went in, oh yes. But I got scared because I don't know what that entrance opens onto. And I'd never let myself be carried off, unless I knew where to.

Yesterday, however, I lost my human setup for hours and hours. If I have the courage, I'll let myself stay lost. But I'm afraid of newness and I'm afraid of living whatever I don't understand—I always want to be sure to at least think I understand, I don't know how to give myself over to disorientation. How could I explain that my greatest fear is precisely of: being? and yet there is no other way. How can I explain that my greatest fear is living whatever comes? how to explain that I can't stand seeing, just because life isn't what I thought but something else—as if I knew what! Why is seeing such disorganization?

And a disappointment. But disappointment with what? if, without even feeling it, I must have hardly been able to stand my barely constructed organization? Maybe disappointment is the fear of no longer belonging to a system. So I could put it like this: he is very happy because he was finally disappointed. What I used to be, was no good for me. But it was from that not-good that I'd organized the best thing of all: hope. From my own flaw I had created a future good. Am I afraid now that my new way of being doesn't make sense? But why not let myself be carried away by whatever happens? I would have to take the holy risk of chance. And I will substitute fate for probability.

But will the discoveries of childhood have been like in a laboratory where you find whatever you find? So it was only as an adult that I grew scared and created the third leg? But as an adult can I find the childish courage to get lost? getting lost means finding things without any idea of what to do with what you're finding. The two legs walking, without the third that holds you back. And I want to be held back. I don't know what to do with the terrifying freedom that could destroy me. But was I happy while imprisoned? or was there, and there was, something restless and sly in my happy jailhouse routine? or was there, and there was, that throbbing thing I was so used to that I thought that throbbing was being a person. Is that right? that too, that too.

I get so scared when I realize I lost my human form for several hours. I don't know if I'll have another form to replace the one I lost. I know I'll need to be careful not to use furtively a new third leg that from me sprouts swiftly as weeds, and to call this protective leg "a truth."

But I also don't know what form to give what happened to me. And without giving it a form, nothing can exist for me. And—and if it's really true that nothing existed?! maybe nothing happened to me? I can only understand what happens to me but things only happen that I understand—what do I know of the rest? the rest didn't exist. Maybe nothing ever existed! Maybe all that happened to me was a slow and great dissolution? And that this is my struggle against that disintegration: trying now to give it a form? A form shapes the chaos, a form gives construction to the amorphous substance—the vision of an infinite piece of meat is the vision of the mad, but if I cut that meat into pieces and parcel them out over days and over hungers—then it would no longer be perdition and madness: it would once again be humanized life.

Humanized life. I had humanized life too much.

But what do I do now? Should I cling to the whole vision, even if that means having an incomprehensible truth? or do I give a form to the nothing, and that would be my attempt to integrate within me my own disintegration? But I'm so little prepared to understand. Before, whenever I tried, my limitations gave me a physical sensation of discomfort, any beginning of thought immediately banged into my forehead. Early on I had to recognize, without complaint, the limits of my small intelligence, and I strayed from the path. I knew I was destined to think little, reasoning kept me confined inside my own skin. So how was I supposed to inaugurate thinking within me now? and maybe only thought can save me, I'm afraid of passion.

Since I must save the day of tomorrow, since I must have a form because I don't feel strong enough to stay disorganized, since I inevitably must slice off the infinite monstrous meat and cut it into pieces the size of my mouth and the size of the vision of my eyes, since I'll inevitably succumb to the need for form that comes from my terror of remaining undelimited— then may I at least have the courage to let this shape form by itself like a scab that hardens by itself, like the fiery nebula that cools into earth. And may I have the great courage to resist the temptation of to invent a form.

This effort I'm making now to let a meaning surface, any meaning, this effort would be easier if I pretended to write to someone.

But I'm afraid to begin composing in order to be understood by the imaginary someone, I'm afraid to start to "make" a meaning, with the same tame madness that till yesterday was my healthy way of fitting into a system. Will I need the courage to use an unprotected heart and keep talking to the nothing and the no one? as a child thinks about the nothing. And run the risk of being crushed by chance.

I don't understand what I saw. And I don't even know if I saw it, since my eyes can't differentiate themselves from the things they see. Only an unexpected tremor of lines, only an anomaly in the uninterrupted continuity of my civilization, made me experience for an instant vitalizing death. The fine death that let me brush up against the forbidden fabric of life. It's forbidden to say the name of life. And I almost said it. I almost couldn't untangle myself from its fabric, which would be the destruction of my age within me.

Perhaps what happened to me was an understanding—and for me to be true, I have to keep on being unable to grasp it, keep on not understanding it. All sudden understanding closely resembles an acute incomprehension.

No. All sudden understanding is finally the revelation of an acute incomprehension. Each moment of finding is a getting lost. Maybe what happened to me was an understanding as complete as an ignorance, and from it I shall emerge as untouched and innocent as before. No understanding of mine will ever reach that knowledge, since living is the only height within my grasp—I am only on the level of life. Except now, now I know a secret. Which I am already forgetting, ah I feel that I am already forgetting....

To learn it again, I would now have to re-die. And knowing might be the murder of my human soul. And I don't want that, I don't. Handing myself over to a new ignorance could save me, possibly. Since as I struggle to know, my new ignorance, which is forgetting, became sacrèd. I'm the vestal priestess of a secret I have forgotten. And I serve the forgotten danger. I found out something I could not understand, my lips were sealed, and all I've got are the incomprehensible fragments of a ritual. Yet for the first time I feel that my forgetting is finally on a level with the world. Ah, and I don't even want anything explained to me that in order to be explained would have to be removed from itself. I don't want anything explained to me that once again needs human validation to be interpreted.

Life and death were mine, and I was monstrous. I was courageous like a sleepwalker who simply goes. During the hours of perdition I had the courage not to compose or organize. And above all not to look ahead. I'd never before had the cour-

8

age to let myself be guided by the unknown and toward the unknown: my expectations preconditioned what I would see. They weren't previsions of a vision: they were already the size of my concerns. My expectations closed the world to me.

Until for several hours I gave up. And, my God, I got what I didn't want. I didn't wander through a river valley—I had always thought that finding would be fertile and moist as a river valley. I didn't realize it was the great un-finding.

To continue being human will my sacrifice be forgetting? Now I'll know how to recognize in the common faces of a few people that—that they forgot. And no longer know that they forgot what they forgot.

I saw. I know I saw because I didn't give my meaning to what I saw. I know I saw—because I don't understand. I know I saw—because there's no point to what I saw. Listen, I'm going to have to speak because I don't know what to do with having lived. Even worse: I don't want what I saw. What I saw smashes my daily life. Sorry for giving you this, I'd much rather have seen something better. Take what I saw, deliver me from my useless vision, and from my useless sin.

I am so afraid that I can only accept that I got lost if I imagine that someone is holding my hand.

Holding someone's hand was always my idea of joy. Often before falling asleep—in that small struggle not to lose consciousness and enter the greater world—often, before having the courage to go toward the greatness of sleep, I pretend that someone is holding my hand and I go, go toward the enormous absence of form that is sleep. And when even then I can't find the courage, then I dream.

Going to sleep so closely resembles the way I now must go

toward my freedom. Handing myself over to what I don't understand would be placing myself at the edge of the nothing. It will be just going, and like a blind woman lost in a field. That supernatural thing which is life. Life that I had tamed to make it familiar. That brave thing that will be handing myself over, and which is like grasping the haunted hand of the God, and entering that formless thing that is a paradise. A paradise that I don't want!

While writing and speaking I will have to pretend that someone is holding my hand.

Oh, at least at the beginning, just at the beginning. As soon as I can let go, I will go alone. In the meantime I must hold this hand of yours—though I can't invent your face and your eyes and your mouth. Yet even amputated, that hand doesn't scare me. Its invention comes from such an idea of love as if the hand really were attached to a body that I don't see only because I can't love enough. I cannot imagine a whole person because I am not a whole person. And how can I imagine a face without knowing what expression I need? As soon as I can release your warm hand, I'll go alone and with horror. The horror will be my responsibility until the metamorphosis is complete and the horror becomes light. Not the light born of a desire for beauty and moralism, as before without realizing I intended; but the natural light of whatever exists, and it is that natural light that terrorizes me. Though I know that the horror—I am the horror in the face of things.

For now I am inventing your presence, just as one day I won't know how to risk dying alone, dying is the greatest risk of all, I won't know how to enter death and take the first step into the first absence of me—just as in this last and so primary hour I shall invent your unknown presence and with you shall begin to die until I learn all by myself not to exist, and then I shall let you go. For now I cling to you, and your unknown and warm life is my only intimate organization, I who without your hand would feel set loose into the enormous vastness I discovered. Into the vastness of the truth?

But the truth never made sense to me. The truth doesn't make sense! That is why I feared it and fear it. Helpless, I give you everything—so you can make a joyous thing of it. Will speaking to you scare you and make me lose you? but if I don't speak I'll be lost, and in losing myself lose you.

The truth doesn't make sense, the greatness of the world restricts me. What I probably asked for and finally got, left me needy as a child wandering the earth alone. So needy that only the love of the entire universe for me could console me and overwhelm me, only a love that trembled the very egg-cell of things with what I am calling a love. With what I can really only call but without knowing its name.

Could what I saw have been love? But what love is as blind as that of an egg-cell? was that it? that horror, was that love? a love so neutral that—no, I still don't want to speak to myself, speaking now would hasten a meaning like someone swiftly freezing into the paralyzing security of a third leg. Or am I just putting off starting to speak? why don't I just say nothing and simply buy some time? Out of fear. I need courage to venture making something concrete out of my feeling. It's like having a coin and not knowing in which country it is legal tender.

I shall need courage to do what I'm about to do: speak. And risk the enormous surprise I shall feel at the poverty of the spoken thing. As soon as it's out of my mouth, I'll have to add: that's not it, that's not it! But I cannot be afraid of being ridiculous, I always preferred less to more also out of fear of the ridiculous: because there's also the shattering of modesty. I'm putting off having to speak to myself. Out of fear?

And because I don't have a word to say.

I don't have a word to say. So why don't I shut up? But if I do not force out the word muteness will swallow me forever in waves. Word and form will be the board upon which I float atop billows of muteness.

And if I'm putting off the beginning it's also because I don't have a guide. The account of other travelers offers me few facts about the voyage: all the information is terribly incomplete.

I feel a first freedom seizing me little by little…. Since until today I never had so little fear of lacking good taste: I wrote "billows of muteness," which I never would have said before because I've always respected beauty and its intrinsic moderation. I said "billows of muteness," my heart bows humbly, and I accept it. Have I finally lost a whole system of good taste? But is that all I've gained? I must have lived so imprisoned to feel freer now just because I no longer fear the lack of aesthetics…. I still can't tell what else I gained. Slowly, perhaps, I'll figure it out. For now the first timid pleasure I am having is realizing I lost my fear of ugliness. And that loss is such goodness. It is a sweetness.

I want to know what else, in losing, I gained. I don't know yet: only by reliving myself shall I live.

But how to relive myself? If I don't have a natural word to say. Will I have to make the word as if creating whatever happened to me?

I shall create whatever happened to me. Only because life cannot be retold. Life is not livable. I shall have to create atop life. And without lying. Create yes, lie no. Creating isn't imagination, it's taking the great risk of grasping reality. Understanding is a creation, my only way. I'll have to make the effort to translate telegraph signals—to translate the unknown into a language I don't speak, and without even understanding what the signals mean. I shall speak that sleepwalker's language that would not be a language if I were awake.

Until I create the truth of what happened to me. Ah, it will be more like scratching than writing, since I'm attempting a reproduction more than an expression. I need to express myself less and less. Is that something else I lost? No, even when making sculptures I was already trying only to reproduce, and only with my hands.

Will I get lost amidst the muteness of the signs? I will, because I know how I am: I could never see without immediately having to do more than see. I know I'll be horrified like a blind person who finally opened her eyes to see—but see what? a mute and incomprehensible triangle. Could that person consider herself no longer blind just because she could see an incomprehensible triangle?

I wonder: if I peer at the darkness with a magnifying glass, will I see more than darkness? the glass doesn't expose the darkness, it only reveals more of it. And if I look at light with a magnifying glass, with a shock I will only see more light. I saw but am as blind as before because I saw an incomprehensible triangle. Unless I too transform myself into the triangle that will recognize in the incomprehensible triangle my own source and repetition.

I'm putting it off. I know that everything I'm saying is just to put it off—to put off the moment when I will have to start to speak, knowing I've got nothing left to say. I'm putting off my silence. Have I done that my entire life? but now, out of disdain for the word, perhaps at last I can begin to speak.

The telegraph signals. The world bristling with antennas,

and I picking up the signal. I can only make the phonetic transcription. Three thousand years ago I went astray, and what was left were phonetic fragments of me. I'm blinder than before. I saw, I did. I saw, and was frightened by the brute truth of a world whose greatest horror is that it is so alive that, in admitting I'm as alive as it is—and my worst discovery is that I'm as alive as it is—I shall have to heighten my consciousness of exterior life until it becomes a crime against my personal life.

For my previous profound morality—my morality was the desire to understand and, since I didn't, I arranged things, this was only yesterday and now I've discovered that I was always profoundly moral: I only admitted the purpose—for my previous profound morality, having discovered that I'm as crudely alive as that crude light I learned yesterday, for that morality of mine, the hard glory of being alive is the horror. Before I lived in the humanized world, but did something purely alive collapse the morality I had?

Because a world fully alive has the power of a Hell.

BECAUSE A WORLD FULLY ALIVE HAS THE POWER OF A Hell.

Yesterday morning—when I left the living room to enter the maid's room—nothing led me to suspect that I was a step away from discovering an empire. Just a step from me. My most primary struggle for the most primary life would open with the calm, devouring ferocity of desert animals. I would encounter inside myself a degree of life so primal in myself that it was nearly inanimate. Yet no gesture of mine hinted that I, with my lips dry from thirst, would come to exist.

Only afterward did an old sentence occur to me, one that years before had been unwittingly engraved upon my memory, no more than the subtitle of a magazine article I ended up not reading: "Lost in the Fiery Hell of a Canyon a Woman Struggles Desperately for Life." Nothing led me to guess where I was going. But then I was never one to recognize events as they were unfolding; every time they came to a head, they surprised me like a break, explosion of instants, with a date, and not the continuation of an uninterruption.

That morning, before entering the maid's room, what was I? I was what others had always seen me be, and that was how I knew myself. I don't know how to say what I was. But at least I want to remember: what was I doing?

It was almost ten in the morning, and for a long time my apartment hadn't much belonged to me. The maid had quit the day before. The fact that nobody was talking or walking and making things happen expanded in silence that house where in semi-luxury I live. I lingered at the breakfast table—how difficult it's being to know what I was like. Yet I must try to at least give myself a prior form in order to understand what happened when I lost that form.

I was lingering at the breakfast table, making balls out of the soft center of a loaf of bread—was that it? I need to know, I need to know what I was! I was this: I was distractedly forming balls out of bread, and my last relaxed romantic entanglement had dissolved amicably with a caress, I gaining once again the happy and somewhat insipid taste of freedom. Does that place me? I'm easy to get along with, I have sincere friendships, and my awareness of this allows me a pleasant friendship with myself, one that has never ruled out a certain ironic feeling for myself, though without persecutions.

But—what my silence was like before, that I don't know and never knew. Sometimes, looking at a snapshot taken on the beach or at a party, I noted with light ironic dread what that smiling, darkened face revealed to me: a silence. A silence and a destiny that escaped me, I, hieroglyphic fragment of an empire dead or alive. Looking at the picture I saw the mystery. No. I'm going to lose the rest of my fear of bad taste, I'm going to begin my exercise in courage, courage isn't being alive, knowing that you're alive is courage—and say that in my photograph I saw The Mystery. The surprise crept up gently, I'm only realizing now that it was the surprise that was creeping up upon me: for in those beaming eyes there was a silence that I'd only seen in lakes, and that I'd only heard in silence itself.

I'd never then imagined that one day I'd go off to encounter that silence. To the shattering of the silence. I glanced at the photographed face and, for a second, in that inexpressive face the world peered back at me just as inexpressive. Was that—just that—my closest contact with myself? the greatest mute depth I could reach, my blindest and most direct link with the world. The rest—the rest were the always organizations of myself, now I know, ah, now I know. The rest was the way I'd transformed myself little by little into the person who bears my name. And I ended up being my name. All you have to do is see the initials G. H. in the leather of my suitcases, and there I am. Neither did I require of others more than the primary covering of their initials. Besides which "psychology" never interested me. The psychological viewpoint made me impatient and still does, it's an instrument that merely trespasses. I think I'd left the psychological stage in adolescence.

G. H. had lived a good bit, by which I mean, had lived many facts. Perhaps I was in some kind of rush to live everything there was to live all at once so I'd have time left over to … to live without facts? to live. Early on I satisfied the duties of my senses, early and quickly I had my sorrows and joys—in order to be quickly freed from my minor human destiny? and be free to go in search of my tragedy.

My tragedy was somewhere. Where was my greater destiny? one that wasn't just the story of my life. Tragedy—which is the greatest adventure—would never happen to me. All I knew was my personal destiny. And what I wanted.

I exude the calm that comes from reaching the point of being G. H. even on my suitcases. Also for my so-called inner life I'd unconsciously adopted my reputation: I treat myself as others treat me, I am whatever others see of me. When I was alone, there was no break, only slightly less of what I was in company, and that had always been my nature and my health. And my kind of beauty. Were my snapshots the only things that photographed an abyss? an abyss.

An abyss of nothing. Just that great and empty thing: an abyss.

I act like a so-called successful person. Having done sculpture for an undetermined and intermittent period also gave me a past and a present that allowed others to situate me: people refer to me as someone who does sculptures that wouldn't be bad if they were less amateurish. For a woman this reputation means a lot socially, and placed me, for others as for myself, in a region that is socially between women and men. Which granted me far more freedom to be a woman, since I didn't have to take formal care to be one.

As for my so-called personal life, maybe it was the sporadic sculpture that gave it a light tone of pre-climax—maybe because of the use of a certain kind of attention that even dilettante art demands. Or because of having the experience of patiently wearing down the material until gradually finding its immanent sculpture; or because of having, also through sculpture, the forced objectivity of dealing with something that was no longer myself.

All this gave me the light tone of pre-climax of someone who knows that, if I get to the bottom of objects, something of those objects will be given to me and in turn given back to the objects. Maybe it was that tone of pre-climax that I saw in the smiling haunted photograph of a face whose word is an inexpressive silence, every picture of a person is a picture of Mona Lisa.

And is that all I can say for myself? That I'm "sincere"? I am, relatively. I don't lie to create false truths. But I overused truths as a pretext. Truth as a pretext to lie? I could tell myself things that flatter me, and just as easily relate my nasty defects. But I must be careful not to confuse defects with truths. I'm afraid of whatever could lead me to a sincerity: my so-called nobility, which I omit, my so-called nastiness, which I also omit. The more sincere I was, the more I'd be tempted to praise my occasional bouts of nobility and especially my occasional nastiness. Sincerity only wouldn't lead me to boast about my pettiness. That I omit, and not just because I couldn't forgive myself for it, I who have forgiven everything serious and significant in myself. I omit pettiness because confession is often a vanity for me, even the painful confession.

It's not that I want to be pure of vanity, but I need to have the field clear of myself in order to keep going. If I go. Or is not wanting to be vain the worst form of vanity? No, I think I need to look without bothering about the color of my eyes, I need to be exempt from myself in order to see.

And is all that what I was? When I open the door to an unexpected visitor, what I catch in the face of the person seeing me at the door is that they've just surprised in me my light pre-climax. What others get from me is then reflected back onto me, and forms the atmosphere called: "I." The pre-climax was perhaps until now my existence. And the other—the unknown and anonymous—, that other existence of mine that was merely deep, was probably what gave me the assurance of a person who always has in the kitchen a kettle on a low flame: whatever happened, I would always have boiling water.

But the water never boiled. I didn't need violence, I bubbled just enough that the water never boiled or spilled. No, I wasn't acquainted with violence. I had been born without a mission, neither did my nature impose one; and I was always delicate enough not to impose upon myself a role. I didn't impose a role upon myself but I did organize myself to be comprehensible for myself, I wouldn't have been able to stand not finding myself in the phone book. My question, if there was one, was not: "Who am I," but "Who is around me." My cycle was complete: what I lived in the present was already getting ready so I could later understand myself. An eye watched over my life. This eye was probably what I would probably now call truth, now morality, now human law, now God, now me. I lived mostly inside a mirror. Two minutes after my birth I had already lost my origins.

A step from climax, a step before revolution, a step before what's called love. A step before my life—which, due to a kind of reverse magnetism, I hadn't transformed into life; and also out of a desire for order. There's a bad taste to the disorder of living. And I wouldn't have even known, if I'd wanted to, how to transform that latent step into a real one. From the pleasure in a harmonious cohesion, from my greedy and permanently promising pleasure in having but not spending—I didn't need the climax or the revolution or anything more than the pre-love, which is so much happier than love. Was the promise enough for me? A promise was enough for me.

Perhaps this attitude or lack of attitude also came from never having had a husband or children, never needing, as they say, to break into or out of anything: I was continuously free.

Being continuously free was also helped by my easy nature: I eat and drink and sleep easily. And, of course, my freedom also came from being financially independent.

From sculpture, I suppose, I got my knack for only thinking when it was time to think, since I had learned to think only with my hands and when it was time to use them. From my intermittent sculpting I'd also acquired the habit of pleasure, toward which I was naturally inclined: my eyes had handled the form of things so many times that I had increasingly learned the pleasure of it, and taking root within it. I could, with much less than I was, I could already use everything: just as yesterday, at the breakfast table, all I needed, to form round forms from the center of the loaf, was the surface of my fingers and the surface of the bread. In order to have what I had I never needed either pain or talent. What I had wasn't an achievement, it was a gift.

And as for men and women, what was I? I've always had an extremely warm admiration for masculine habits and ways, and I had an unurgent pleasure in being feminine, being feminine was also a gift. All I had was the easiness of gifts, and not the fright of vocations—is that it?

At the table where I lingered because I had the time, I looked around while my fingers rolled the bread into balls. The world was a place. Which suited me for living: in the world I could press one soft ball of bread into another, all I had to do was rub them together and, without too much exertion, just knead them enough to make one surface bind with another, and so with pleasure I was shaping a curious pyramid that satisfied me: a right triangle made of round shapes, a shape that is made of its opposite shapes. If that had any meaning for me, the bread and my fingers probably knew.

The apartment reflects me. It's on the top floor, which is considered an elegance. People of my milieu try to live in the so-called "penthouse." It's much more than an elegance. It's a real pleasure: from there you dominate a city. When this elegance gets too common, will I, without even knowing why, move onto another elegance? Maybe. Like me, the apartment has moist shadows and lights, nothing here is abrupt; one room precedes and promises the next. From my dining room I could see the mixtures of shadows that were a prelude to the living room. Everything here is the elegant, ironic, and witty replica of a life that never existed anywhere: my house is a merely artistic creation.

Everything here actually refers to a life that wouldn't suit me if it were real. What is it imitating, then? If it were real, I wouldn't understand it, but I like the duplicate and understand it. The copy is always pretty. My semi-artistic and artistic milieu should, however, make me disdain copies: but I always seemed to prefer the parody, it was useful to me. Imitating a life probably gave me—or still does? how much has the harmony of my past been ruptured?—, imitating a life probably gave me assurance precisely because that life wasn't my own: it wasn't a responsibility of mine.

The light general pleasure—which seems to have been the tone in which I live or lived—perhaps came from the world's not being either me or mine: I could enjoy it. Just as with the men I hadn't made my own, and whom I could admire and sincerely love, as one loves without egoism, as one loves an idea. Since they weren't mine, I never tortured them.

As one loves an idea. The witty elegance of my house comes from everything here being in quotes. Out of honest respect for true authorship, I quote the world, I quoted it, since it was neither me nor mine. Was beauty, as for everyone, was a certain beauty my goal? did I live in beauty?

As for myself, without lying or being truthful—as at that moment yesterday morning when I was sitting at the breakfast table—as for myself, I always kept a quotation mark to my left and another to my right. Somehow "as if it wasn't me" was broader than if it *were*—an inexistent life possessed me entirely and kept me busy like an invention. Only in photography, when the negative was developed, was something else revealed that, uncaught by me, was caught by the snapshot: when the negative was developed my presence as ectoplasm was revealed too. Is photography the picture of a hollow, of a lack, of an absence?

Whereas I myself, more than clean and correct, was a pretty replica. Since all that was probably what made me generous and pretty. All an experienced man needed was one glance to know that I was a woman of generosity and grace, and one who isn't a bother, and one who doesn't eat away at a man: a woman who smiles and laughs. I respect other people's pleasure, and delicately I consume my own pleasure, tedium nourishes me and delicately consumes me, the sweet tedium of a honeymoon.

That image of myself in quotes satisfied me, and not just superficially. I was the image of what I was not, and that image of not-being overwhelmed me: one of the most powerful states is being negatively. Since I didn't know what I was, "not being" was the closest I could get to the truth: at least I had the other side: I at least had the "not," I had my opposite. I didn't know what was good for me, so I lived a kind of pre-eagerness for my "bad."

And living my "bad," I lived the other side of something I

couldn't even manage to want or attempt. Like somebody who follows with love a life of "whoredom," and at least has the opposite of what she doesn't know or want or have: the life of a nun. Only now do I know that I already had it all, though the other way around: I was devoted to every detail of the not. Painstakingly not being, I was proving to myself that—that I was.

That way of not-being was so much more pleasant, so much cleaner: since, without meaning this ironically, I'm a woman of spirit. And with a spirited body. At the breakfast table I was framed by my white robe, my clean and well-sculpted face, and a simple body. I exuded the kind of goodness that comes from indulging one's own pleasures and those of others. I ate delicately what was mine, and delicately wiped my mouth with the napkin.

This her, G. H. in the leather of her suitcases, was I: is it I—still? No. I immediately figure that the hardest thing my vanity will have to face is the judgment of myself: I'll have every appearance of a failure, and only I will know if that was the failure I needed.

ONLY I WILL KNOW IF THAT WAS THE FAILURE I NEEDED.

I finally got up from the breakfast table, that woman. Not having a maid that day would give me the type of activity I wanted: arranging. I always liked to arrange things. I guess it's my only real vocation. By putting things in order, I create and understand at the same time. But since I gradually, through reasonably good investments, became fairly well-off, that hampered me in my ability to use this vocation of mine: if money and education hadn't put me in the class I belong to, I'd normally have worked as the maid who arranges things in a large home of rich people, where there is so much to arrange. Arranging is finding the best form. If I'd been a maid-arranger, I wouldn't have even needed the amateurism of sculpture; if with my hands I'd been able to arrange things for hours on end. To arrange the form?

The always forbidden pleasure of arranging a house was so great that, still sitting at the table, I was already savoring the feeling in the mere planning of it. I looked around the apartment: where would I begin?

And also so that afterward, in the seventh hour as on the seventh day, I would be free to rest and enjoy the calm remainder of the day. Almost joyless calm, which would be a good balance for me: the hours doing sculpture taught me almost joyless calm. The week before I'd had too much fun, gone out too much, had too much of everything I wanted, and now I wished for a day exactly like the one this one promised to be: heavy and good and empty. I'd stretch it out as long as possible.

Maybe I'd start cleaning at the back of the apartment: the maid's room must be filthy, given its dual roles as a sleeping space and storage room for old clothes, suitcases, ancient newspapers, wrapping paper and leftover twine. I'd clean and ready it for the new maid. Then, from the back, I'd slowly "climb" horizontally until I reached the opposite end of the apartment which was the living room, where—as if I myself were the finish line of the arrangements and of the morning—I'd read the newspaper, stretched out on the sofa, and probably fall asleep. If the telephone didn't ring.

Better yet, I decided to take the phone off the hook and that way I was sure nothing would disturb me.

How can I say now that I'd already begun to see what would only become evident afterward? without knowing it, I was already in the entrance to the room. I was already starting to see, and didn't know it; I had seen since I was born and didn't know, I didn't know.

Give me your unknown hand, since life is hurting me, and I don't know how to speak—reality is too delicate, only reality is delicate, my unreality and my imagination are heavier.

Having decided to begin with the maid's room, I crossed the kitchen that leads to the service area. At the end of the service area is the hallway to the maid's room. First, though, I leaned against the wall in the hallway to finish a cigarette.

I looked down: thirteen floors fell away from the building. I didn't know that all this was already part of what was about to happen. A thousand times before this the movement must have started and then was lost. This time the movement would go all the way though, and I didn't see it coming.

I looked around the courtyard, the backs of all the apartments from which my apartment too looked like a back. On the outside my building was white, with the smoothness of marble and the smoothness of surface. But the courtyard was a heap of frames, windows, riggings and blackened watermarks, window straddling window, mouths peering into mouths. The belly of my building was like a factory. The miniature of the grandeur of a panorama full of gorges and canyons: smoking there, as if on a mountaintop, I was looking at the view, probably with the same inexpressive look I had in my photographs.

I saw what it was saying: it was saying nothing. And I was taking this nothing in attentively, I was taking it in with what was inside my eyes in the photographs; only now do I know that I was always receiving the mute signal. I looked around the courtyard. Everything was of an inanimate richness that recalled that of nature: there too one could mine uranium and from there oil could gush.

I was seeing something that would only make sense later—I mean, something that only later would profoundly not make sense. Only later would I understand: what seems like a lack of meaning—that's the meaning. Every moment of "lack of meaning" is precisely the frightening certainty that that's exactly what it means, and that not only can I not reach it, I don't want to because I have no guarantees. The lack of meaning would only overwhelm me later. Could realizing the lack of meaning have always been my negative way of sensing the meaning? it had been my way of participating.

What I was seeing in the monstrous insides of that machine, which was the courtyard of my building, what I was seeing were made things, eminently practical things and with a practical purpose.

But something of the terrible general nature—which I would later experience within myself—something of inescapable nature would inescapably leave the hands of the hundred or so practical workmen who had labored on the drainpipes, entirely unaware that they were erecting that Egyptian ruin that I was now regarding with the gaze of my beach pictures. Only later would I know that I'd seen; only later, when I saw the secret, would I realize I'd already seen it.

I threw my lit cigarette over the edge, and stepped back, slyly hoping none of the neighbors would connect me with the act forbidden by the administrators of the Building. Then, carefully, I stuck out just my head, and looked: I couldn't even guess where the cigarette had landed. The precipice had swallowed it in silence. Was I there thinking? at least I was thinking about nothing. Or maybe about whether some neighbor had seen me commit that forbidden act, which above all didn't match the polite woman I am, which made me smile.

Then I headed into the dark hallway behind the service area.

THEN I HEADED INTO THE DARK HALLWAY BEHIND THE service area.

In the hall, which forms the end of the apartment, two doors, indistinct in the shadows, face: the service exit and the door to the maid's room. The *bas-fond* of my house. I opened the door onto the pile of newspapers and the darknesses of dirt and of the junk.

But when I opened the door my eyes winced in reverberations and physical displeasure.

Because instead of the confused murk I was expecting, I bumped into the vision of a room that was a quadrilateral of white light; my eyes protected themselves by squinting.

For around six months—the amount of time that maid had been with me—I hadn't gone in there, and my astonishment came from coming into an entirely clean room.

I'd expected to find darknesses, I'd been prepared to throw open the window and clean out the dank darkness with fresh air. I hadn't expected the maid, without a word to me, to have arranged the room in her own way, stripping it of its storage function as brazenly as if she owned it.

From the doorway I was now seeing a room that had a calm and empty order. In my fresh, damp and cozy home, the maid without telling me had opened a dry emptiness. Now it was an entirely clean and vibrant room as in an insane asylum from which dangerous objects have been removed.

There, because of the created void, were concentrated the reverberation of the tiles, the cement terraces, the erect antennas of all the neighboring buildings, and the reflection of their thousand windowpanes. The room seemed to be on a level incomparably higher than the apartment itself.

Like a minaret. So began my first impression of a minaret, free above a limitless expanse. That impression was the only way I could for the time being perceive my physical displeasure.

The room was not a regular quadrilateral: two of its angles were slightly more open. And though that was its material reality, it came to me as if it were my vision that was deforming it. It looked like the representation, on paper, of the way I could see a quadrilateral: already deformed in its perspective lines. The solidification of a flaw in vision, the concretization of an optical illusion. Its not entirely regular angles made it appear fundamentally fragile as if the room-minaret were not implanted in either the apartment or the building.

From the doorway I saw the steady sun cutting half of the ceiling and a third of the floor with a neat line of black shadow. For six months a permanent sun had warped the pine wardrobe, and stripped the whitewash to an even whiter white.

And it was on one of the walls that flinching with surprise I saw the unexpected mural.

On the whitewashed wall, beside the door—and that's why I hadn't seen it—were nearly life-sized charcoal outlines of a naked man, a naked woman, and a dog that was more naked than a dog. Upon the bodies nothing was drawn of what nakedness reveals, the nakedness simply came from the absence of everything that covers it: they were the outlines of an empty nakedness. The lines were coarse, made with a broken-tipped piece of charcoal. Some strokes were doubled as if one line were the trembling of the other. A dry trembling of dry charcoal.

The rigidity of the lines pegged the blown-up and doltish figures on the wall, like three automatons. Even the dog had the mild madness of something that doesn't move by its own strength. The coarseness of the excessively firm line made the dog something solid and petrified, more pegged to itself than to the wall.

After the initial surprise of discovering the hidden mural in my own house, I examined more closely, this time with amused surprise, the figures sprung upon the wall. Their simplified feet didn't quite touch the floor, their small heads didn't touch the ceiling—and that, together with the stupefied rigidity of the lines, left the three figures loose like the ghosts of three mummies. The more uncomfortable their hard motionlessness made me, the more they reminded me of mummies. They were emerging as if they'd gradually oozed from the wall, slowly coming from the center until they'd sweated through the rough lime surface.

None of the figures was connected, and the three did not form a group: each figure looked forward, as if they'd never looked to the side, as if they'd never seen each other and didn't know anyone existed beside them.

I smiled uncomfortably, I was trying to smile: because each figure was there on the wall exactly as I myself had stood rigidly in the doorway. The drawing wasn't a decoration: it was a writing.

The memory of the absent maid constrained me. I wanted to remember her face, and to my astonishment couldn't—she'd managed to exclude me from my own house, as if she'd shut the door and left me a stranger to my own dwelling. The recollection of her face escaped me, it had to be a temporary lapse.

But her name—right, right, I finally remembered: Janair. And, looking at the hieratic drawing, it suddenly occurred to me that Janair despised me. I was looking at the figures of the man and woman with the palms of their forceful hands open and exposed, and who seemed to have been left there by Janair as a crude message for when I opened the door.

In a way my discomfort was amusing: it had never occurred to me that, in Janair's muteness, there might have been a reprimand of my life, which her silence might have called "a wanton life"? how had she judged me?

I looked at the mural where I was likely depicted ... I, the Man. And as for the dog—was that the epithet she gave me? For years I had only been judged by my peers and by my own milieu that was, as a whole, made of myself and for myself. Janair was the first truly outside person of whose gaze I was becoming aware.

Abruptly, this time with real discomfort, I finally let a sensation come to me which for six months, out of negligence and lack of interest, I hadn't let myself feel: the silent hatred of that woman. What surprised me was that it was a kind of detached hatred, the worst kind: indifferent hatred. Not a hatred that individualized me but merely the lack of mercy. No, not even hatred.

That was when I unexpectedly managed to remember her face, but of course, how could I have forgotten? I saw her black and motionless face again, saw her wholly opaque skin that seemed more like yet another of her ways of being silent, her extremely well drawn eyebrows, I saw her fine and delicate features barely discernible against the closed-off blackness of her skin.

Her features—I discovered without pleasure—were the features of a queen. And her posture too: her body erect, thin, hard, smooth, almost fleshless, lacking breasts or hips. And her clothes? It wasn't surprising that I'd used her as if she had no presence: beneath her small apron, she always wore dark brown or black, which made her entirely dark and invisible— I shivered to discover that until now I hadn't noticed that the woman was an invisible person. Janair almost only had an external form, the features within her form were so refined that they hardly existed: she was flat as a bas-relief stuck on a board.

And was it unavoidable that she saw me as she was? abstracting from that body of mine on the wall everything that wasn't essential, and also seeing only my outline. Yet, curiously, the figure on the wall did remind me of someone, and that was myself. Constrained by the presence Janair had left of herself in this room within my house, I sensed the three angular zombie figures had in fact held me back as if the room were still occupied.

I hesitated at the door.

Also because the unexpected simplicity of the dwelling disoriented me: I really didn't even know where to start arranging things, or even if there was anything to arrange.

I looked despondently at the nakedness of the minaret:

The bed, stripped of its sheets, exposed the dusty cloth mattress, with its long faded stains that looked like sweat or watery blood, old and pale stains. The odd fibrous horsehair pierced the cloth of the mattress that was so dry it was rotten, and stuck out erect in the air.

Along one of the walls, three old suitcases were stacked with such perfect symmetry that I hadn't noticed them, since they did nothing to alter the emptiness of the room. Upon them, and upon the nearly dead sign of a "G. H.", an already calm and sedimented accumulation of dust.

And there was also the narrow wardrobe: it had a single door, and was the height of a person, my height. The wood continuously dried by the sun opened in fissures and barbs. So that Janair had never closed the window? She'd taken more advantage than I had of the view from the "penthouse."

The room was so different from the rest of the apartment that going in there was as if I had first left my house and slammed the door. The room was the opposite of what I'd created in my home, the opposite of the soft beauty I'd made from my talent for arrangement, my talent for living, the opposite of my serene irony, of my sweet and absentminded irony: it was a violation of my quotation marks, the quotation marks that made me a citation of myself. The room was the portrait of an empty stomach.

And nothing there was made by me. In the rest of the house the sun filtered from the outside in, ray upon gentle ray, the result of my employment of both heavy and light curtains. But here the sun didn't seem to come from outside: it was the sun's own place, fixed and unmoving, in a harsh light as if it never shut its eyes even at night. Everything there was sliced-up nerves that had been hung up and dried on a clothesline. I was prepared to clean dirty things but dealing with that absence disoriented me.

I realized then that I was irritated. The room was making me physically uncomfortable as if the air still contained the sound of dry charcoal scratching the dry lime. The room's inaudible sound was like a needle sweeping across a record after the music has stopped. A neutral hissing of thing was what made up the substance of its silence. Charcoal and fingernail coming together, charcoal and fingernail, calm and compact rage of that woman who represented a silence as though representing a foreign country, the African queen. And she'd been lodging there inside my house, the foreigner, the indifferent enemy.

I wondered if Janair had really despised me—or if I, who hadn't even looked at her, had been the one who despised her. Just as I was discovering now with irritation that the room didn't just irritate me, I detested it, that cubicle with nothing but surfaces: its entrails had been parched. I looked at it with disgust and disappointment.

Until I forced myself to summon some courage and a violence: on this very day everything there would have to be altered.

First I'd drag the few things inside the room into the hallway. And then I'd throw into the empty room bucket upon bucket of water that the hard air would swallow, and then I'd swamp the dust until a moistness was finally born in that desert, destroying the minaret that haughtily overlooked a horizon of rooftops. I'd throw water into the wardrobe to flood it up to its mouth—and then at last, at last I'd see the wood start to rot. An inexplicable rage, but which came naturally, overwhelmed me: I wanted to kill something there.

And then, then I'd cover that dried-out straw mattress with a soft, clean, cold sheet, one of my own sheets with my embroidered initials, replacing the one Janair must have thrown in the wash.

But first I'd scrape the gritty dryness of the charcoal off the wall, I'd carve off the dog with a knife, erasing the exposed palms of the man, destroying the too-small head of that large naked woman. And I'd throw water and water that would run in rivers down the scraped-down wall.

As if already seeing a picture of the room after being transformed into me and mine, I sighed with relief.

I then went in.

How to explain, except that something I don't understand was happening. What did she want, that woman who is me? what was happening to a G. H. on the leather of her suitcases?

Nothing, nothing, only that my nerves were now awake—my nerves that had been calm or simply arranged? had my silence been a silence or a high mute voice?

How can I explain it to you: suddenly the whole world that was me shriveled up in fatigue, I could no longer bear on my shoulders—what?—and was succumbing to a tension that I didn't know had always been mine. They were already starting, and I still didn't realize it, the first signs inside me of a landslide, of underground limestone caves, collapsing beneath the weight of stratified archeological layers—and the weight of the first landslide was bringing down the corners of my mouth, making my arms fall. What was happening to me? I'll never understand but there must be someone who understands. And it's inside myself that I must create that someone who will understand.

And though I'd gone into the room, I seemed to have gone into nothing. Even once inside it, I was still somehow outside. As if the room weren't deep enough to hold me and I had to leave pieces of myself in the hallway, in the worst rejection to which I'd ever fallen victim: I didn't fit.

At the same time, looking at the low sky of the whitewashed ceiling, I was feeling suffocated by confinement and restriction. And I was already longing for my house. I forced myself to remember that that room too was my possession, and inside my house: I'd walked to the room without leaving my apartment, without going upstairs or down. Unless one could fall into a well horizontally, as if they'd slightly warped the building and I, slipping, had been tossed from door to door until reaching this highest one of all.

Caught there in a web of vacancies, I once again forgot the plan I'd outlined for arranging the room, and wasn't sure where to begin. The room didn't have a point that could be called its beginning, nor one that could be considered its end. It had a sameness that made it endless.

I ran my eyes over the wardrobe, lifted them toward a crack in the ceiling, trying to get a slightly better grip on that vast emptiness. With more daring, though without the slightest intimacy, I ran my fingers over the bunched-up cloth atop the mattress.

I got excited by an idea: the wardrobe, well-nourished with water, its fibers gorged, could be polished until it shined, and I would wax the inside too, since the interior was probably even more scorched.

I cracked the wardrobe's narrow door, and the darkness inside escaped like a puff. I tried to open it a bit more, but the door was blocked by the foot of the bed, which it was knocking up against. Inside the breach, I put as much of my face as I could fit. And, as if the darkness inside were spying on me, we briefly spied each other without seeing each other. I saw nothing, only managing to whiff the dry, burnt odor like the smell of a live hen. Yet by pushing the bed closer to the window, I managed to open the door a few centimeters more.

Then, before understanding, my heart went gray as hair goes gray.

THEN, BEFORE UNDERSTANDING, MY HEART WENT gray as hair goes gray.

Meeting the face I had put inside the opening, right near my eyes, in the half-darkness, the fat cockroach had moved. My cry was so muffled that only the contrasting silence let me know I hadn't screamed. The scream had stayed beating in my chest.

Nothing, it was nothing—I immediately tried to calm down from my fright. I'd never expected in a house meticulously disinfected against my disgust for cockroaches that this room had escaped. No, it was nothing. It was a cockroach that was slowly moving toward the gap.

From its bulk and slowness, it had to be a very old cockroach. With my archaic horror of cockroaches I'd learned to guess, even from a distance, their ages and dangers; even without ever having really looked a cockroach in the face I knew the ways they existed.

It was just that discovering sudden life in the nakedness of the room had startled me as if I'd discovered that the dead room was in fact mighty. Everything there had dried up—but a cockroach remained. A cockroach so old that it was immemorial. What I had always found repulsive in roaches is that they were obsolete yet still here. Knowing that they were already on the Earth, and the same as they are today, even before the first dinosaurs appeared, knowing the first man already found them proliferated and crawling alive, knowing that they had witnessed the formation of the great deposits of oil and coal in the world, and there they were during the great advance and then during the great retreat of the glaciers—the peaceful resistance. I knew that roaches could endure for more than a month without food or water. And that they could even make a usable nutritive substance from wood. And that, even after being crushed, they slowly decompressed and kept on walking. Even when frozen, they kept on marching once thawed.... For three hundred and fifty million years they had been replicating themselves without being transformed. When the world was nearly naked, they were already sluggishly covering it.

Like there, in the naked and parched room, the virulent drop: in the clean test-tube a drop of matter.

I looked at the room with distrust. So there was a roach. Or roaches. Where? behind the suitcases perhaps. One? two? how many? Behind the motionless silence of the suitcases, perhaps a whole darkness of roaches. Each immobilized atop another? Layers of roaches—which all of a sudden reminded me what I'd discovered as a child when I lifted the mattress I slept on: the blackness of hundreds and hundreds of bedbugs, crowded together one atop the other.

The memory of my childhood poverty, with bedbugs, leaky roofs, cockroaches and rats, was like that of my prehistoric past, I had already lived with the first creatures of the Earth.

One cockroach? many? how many?! I asked myself in a

rage. I let my gaze wander over the naked room. No sound, no sign: but how many? No sound and yet I distinctly felt an emphatic resonance, which was that of silence chafing against silence. Hostility overwhelmed me. It's more than just not liking roaches: I don't want them. Besides which they're the miniature version of an enormous animal. My hostility was growing.

It wasn't I who spurned the room, as I'd felt for a moment at the door. The room, with its secret cockroach, had spurned me. At first I'd been rejected by a vision of a nakedness as powerful as that of a mirage; though what I'd seen wasn't the mirage of an oasis, but the mirage of a desert. Then I'd been immobilized by the hard message on the wall: the open-palmed figures had been one of the successive sentries at the entrance to the sarcophagus. And now I was understanding that the roach and Janair were the true inhabitants of the room.

No, I wouldn't arrange anything—not if there were roaches. The new maid would devote her first day at work to that dusty and empty hutch.

A wave of goose bumps, inside the great heat of the sun, covered me: I rushed to get out of the blazing room.

My first physical movement of fear, finally expressed, was what revealed to me to my surprise that I was fearful. And it ushered me into an even greater fear—when I tried to leave, I tripped between the foot of the bed and the wardrobe. A possible fall in that room of silence caused my body to shrink back in profound revulsion—tripping had made my attempt to flee an abortive act in itself—could this be how "they," the ones by the sarcophagus, had of preventing me from ever leaving again? They had kept me from leaving and just in this simple way: they left me entirely free, since they knew I could no longer leave without tripping and falling.

I wasn't imprisoned but I was located. As located as if they'd stuck me there with the simple and single gesture of pointing at me with a finger, pointing at me and at a place.

I'd already known the feeling of place. As a child, I unexpectedly became aware of lying in a bed located in a city located on the Earth located in the World. As in childhood, I then had the strong sense that I was entirely alone in a house, and that the house was high and floating in the air, and that the house had invisible roaches.

Before, when I'd located myself, I'd be magnified. Now I located myself with limits—limiting myself to the point that, inside the room, the only place for me was between the foot of the bed and the wardrobe door.

Only now the feeling of place was luckily not coming to me at night, as in childhood, since it must have been around ten in the morning.

And unexpectedly the approaching eleven o'clock seemed to me an element of terror—like the place, time too had become palpable, it was like wanting to flee from inside a clock, and I hurried wildly.

But to be able to leave the corner where, having cracked the wardrobe door, I'd blocked myself in, I'd first have to shut the door pinning me to the foot of the bed: there I had no free path, trapped by the sun that was now burning the hairs on the nape of my neck, in the dry oven called ten a.m.

My quick hand went to the wardrobe door to shut it and make way for me—but I withdrew again.

Because inside the cockroach had moved.

I quieted down. My breath was light, superficial. I now felt there was no going back. And I already knew that, absurd as it may seem, my only chance of getting out of there was by admitting head-on and absurdly that something was becoming irremediable. I knew I had to admit the danger I was in, even though I was aware that it was madness to believe in an entirely nonexistent danger. But I had to believe in myself—my whole life just like everybody else I'd been in danger—but now, in order to leave, I had the delirious responsibility of having to know it.

Penned between the wardrobe door and the foot of the bed, I still hadn't tried to move my feet again, drawing back instead as if, even in its extreme slowness, the roach might spring forward—I'd seen roaches who suddenly fly, the winged fauna.

I stayed still, calculating wildly. I was alert, I was totally alert. Inside me a feeling of intense expectation had grown, and a surprised resignation: because in this state of alert expectation I was seeing all my earlier expectations, I was seeing the awareness from which I'd also lived before, an awareness that never leaves me and that in the final analysis might be the thing that most attached to my life—perhaps that awareness was my life itself. The cockroach too: what's the only feeling a cockroach has? the awareness of living, inextricable from its body. In me, everything I had superimposed upon the inextricable part of myself, would probably never manage to stifle the awareness that, more than awareness of life, was the actual process of life inside me.

That was when the cockroach began to emerge.

THAT WAS WHEN THE COCKROACH BEGAN TO EMERGE.

First the heralding quiver of its antennae.

Then, behind those dry stands, the reluctant body started to emerge. Until nearly all of it reached the opening of the wardrobe door.

It was brown, it was hesitant as if of enormous weight. It was now almost entirely visible.

I quickly lowered my eyes. On hiding my eyes, I was hiding from the roach the cunning idea that occurred to me— my heart was beating almost as in a joy. Because I suddenly felt that I had resources, I'd never before used my resources— and now a whole latent power was throbbing inside me, and a greatness was overtaking me: the greatness of courage, as if fear itself had finally invested me with courage. Moments before I had superficially assumed that my only feelings were indignation and disgust, but now I recognized—although I'd never known it before—that what was happening was that I was finally taking on a fear much greater than myself.

This great fear deepened everything within me. Turned

inward into myself, as a blind man sounds out his own attentiveness, for the first time I had wholly fallen back upon an instinct. And I shivered with extreme pleasure as if finally mindful of the grandeur of an instinct that was bad, total and infinitely sweet—as if finally tasting, and within myself, a grandeur greater than myself. I was getting drunk for the first time with a hatred clear as a fountain, drunk with the desire, justified or not, to kill.

A whole lifetime of awareness—for fifteen centuries I hadn't struggled, for fifteen centuries I hadn't killed, for fifteen centuries I hadn't died—a whole lifetime of tamed awareness was now collecting inside me and banging like a mute bell whose vibrations I didn't need to hear, I was recognizing them. As if for the first time I was finally on the level of Nature.

A wholly controlled rapacity had overwhelmed me, and since it was controlled it was all power. Up till then I'd never mastered my own powers—powers I neither understood nor wanted to understand, but the life inside me had hung on to them so that one day at last this unknown and happy and unconscious matter would unclasp what was finally: I! I, whatever that was.

Brazenly, stirred by my surrender to what is evil, brazenly, stirred, grateful, for the first time I was being the unknown person I was—except that not knowing myself would no longer keep me back, the truth had already surpassed me: I lifted my hand as if to swear an oath, and in a single blow slammed the door on the half-emerged body of the cockroach———

————

As I did I had also closed my eyes. And that's how I remained, trembling all over. What had I done?

Maybe then I already knew that I didn't mean what had I done to the cockroach but: what had I done to myself?

Because during those seconds, eyes shut, I was becoming aware of myself as one becomes aware of a taste: all of me tasted of steel and verdigris, I was all acid like metal on the tongue, like a crushed green plant, my whole taste rose to my mouth. What had I done to myself? With my heart thumping, my temples pulsing, this is what I'd done to myself: I had killed. I had killed! But why such delight, and besides that a vital acceptance of that delight? For how long, then, had I been about to kill?

No, it wasn't about that. The question was: what had I killed?

That calm woman I'd always been, had she gone mad with pleasure? With my eyes still closed I was trembling with delight. To have killed—was so much greater than I was, it was appropriate to that limitless room. To have killed opened the dryness of the sands of the room to dampness, finally, finally, as if I'd dug and dug with hard and eager fingers until I found within myself a thread of drinkable life that was the thread of death. I slowly opened my eyes, with sweetness now, in gratitude, shyness, with a modesty of glory.

From the finally damp world from which I was emerging, I opened my eyes and met the great and harsh open light, I saw the now-closed door of the wardrobe.

And I saw half of the roach's body outside the door.

Sticking out, erect in the air, a caryatid.

But a living caryatid.

I hesitated to comprehend, looking at it in surprise. I gradually realized what had happened: I hadn't slammed the door hard enough. I'd caught the cockroach, yes, which couldn't go any further. But I'd left it alive.

Alive and looking at me. I quickly averted my eyes, with violent revulsion.

I needed, therefore, to strike again. One more strike? I

wasn't looking at the roach, but I told myself I still needed to strike one more time—I repeated it slowly as if each repetition could command the pulses of my heart, the beats that were spaced too widely like the soreness of a pain I couldn't feel.

Until—finally managing to hear myself, finally managing to get myself under control—I lifted my hand high in the air as if my whole body, along with the blow of my arm, would come down against the wardrobe door.

But that was when I saw the roach's face.

It was sticking straight out, at the height of my head and my eyes. For a second I sat there with my hand frozen in the air. Then I gradually lowered it.

A second earlier I might still have been able not to see the countenance on the cockroach's face.

But it happened a fraction of a second too late: I was seeing. My hand, which had lowered when it abandoned its determination to strike, was slowly rising back to stomach-level: though I myself hadn't moved, my stomach had cringed inside my body. My mouth was terribly dry, I ran an equally dry tongue over my rough lips.

It was a face without a contour. The antennae stuck out in whiskers on either side of its mouth. Its brown mouth was well-drawn. The long and slender whiskers were moving slow and dry. Its black faceted eyes were looking. It was a cockroach as old as a fossilized fish. It was a cockroach as old as salamanders and chimeras and griffins and leviathans. It was as ancient as a legend. I looked at its mouth: there was the real mouth.

I had never seen a roach's mouth. I in fact—I had never actually seen a cockroach. I had just been repulsed by its ancient and ever-present existence—but had never actually come face-to-face with one, not even in thought.

And so I was discovering that, though compact, a roach is composed of layers and brown layers, fine as onionskin, as if each could be lifted by a fingernail and still there would always be another underneath, and then another. Maybe the scales were its wings, but then it must be made of layers and layers of thin wings pressed together to form that compact body.

It was reddish-brown. And had cilia all over. Maybe the cilia were its multiple legs. The antennae were now still, dry and dusty strands.

A cockroach doesn't have a nose. I looked at it, with that mouth and eyes: it looked like a dying mulatto woman. But its eyes were radiant and black. The eyes of a bride. Each individual eye looked like a cockroach. The fringed, dark, dustless and living eye. And the other eye was the same. Two roaches implanted in the roach, and each eye reproduced the entire cockroach.

EACH EYE REPRODUCED THE ENTIRE COCKROACH.

—Pardon me for giving you this, hand holding mine, but I don't want this for myself! take that roach, I don't want what I saw.

There I was open-mouthed and offended and withdrawn— faced with the dusty being looking back at me. Take what I saw: because what I was seeing with an embarrassment so painful and so frightened and so innocent, what I was seeing was life looking back at me.

How else could I describe that crude and horrible, raw matter and dry plasma, that was there, as I shrank into myself with dry nausea, I falling centuries and centuries inside a mud—it was mud, and not even dried mud but mud still damp and still alive, it was a mud in which the roots of my identity were still shifting with unbearable slowness.

Take it, take all this for yourself, I don't want to be a living person! I'm disgusted and amazed by myself, thick mud slowly oozing.

That's what it was—so that's what it was. Because I'd

looked at the living roach and was discovering inside it the identity of my deepest life. In a difficult demolition, hard and narrow paths were opening within me.

I looked at it, at the roach: I hated it so much that I was going over to its side, feeling solidarity with it, since I couldn't stand being left alone with my aggression.

And all of a sudden I moaned out loud, this time I heard my moan. Because rising to my surface like pus was my truest matter—and with fright and loathing I was feeling that "I-being" was coming from a source far prior to the human source and, with horror, much greater than the human.

Opening in me, with the slowness of stone doors, opening in me was the wide life of silence, the same that was in the fixed sun, the same that was in the immobilized roach. And that could be the same as in me! if I had the courage to abandon ... to abandon my feelings? If I had the courage to abandon hope.

Hope for what? For the first time I was astonished to feel that I'd based an entire hope on becoming something that I was not. The hope—what other name could I give it?—that for the first time I now was going to abandon, out of courage and mortal curiosity. Had hope, in my prior life, been based upon a truth? With childlike surprise, I was starting to doubt it.

To find out what I really could hope for, would I first have to pass through my truth? To what extent had I invented a destiny now, while subterraneously living from another?

I closed my eyes, waiting for the astonishment to pass, waiting for my panting to calm to the point that it was no longer that awful moan that I'd heard as if coming from the bottom of a dry, deep cistern, as the cockroach was a creature of a dry cistern. I was still feeling, at an incalculable distance within me, that moan that was no longer reaching my throat.

This is madness, I thought with my eyes closed. But it was so undeniable feeling that birth from inside the dust—that all I could do was follow something I was well aware wasn't madness, it was, my God, the worse truth, the horrible one. But why horrible? Because without words it contradicted everything I used to think also without words.

I waited for the astonishment to pass, for health to return. But I was realizing, in an immemorial effort of memory, that I had felt this astonishment before: it was the same one I had experienced when I saw my own blood outside of me, and I had marveled at it. Since the blood I was seeing outside of me, that blood I was drawn to with such wonder: it was mine.

I didn't want to open my eyes, I didn't want to keep on seeing. It was important not to forget the rules and the laws, to remember that without the rules and laws there would be no order, I had to not forget them and defend them in order to defend myself.

But it was already too late for me to hold myself back.

The first bind had already involuntarily burst, and I was breaking loose from the law, though I intuited that I was going to enter the hell of living matter—what kind of hell awaited me? but I had to go. I had to sink into my soul's damnation, curiosity was consuming me.

So I opened my eyes all at once, and saw the full endless vastness of the room, that room that was vibrating in silence, laboratory of hell.

The room, the unknown room. My entrance into it was finally complete.

The entrance to this room had a single passageway, and a narrow one: through the cockroach. The cockroach that was filling the room with finally open vibration, the vibrations of its rattlesnake tails in the desert. Through a painstaking route, I had reached the deep incision in the wall that was that room—and the crevice created a vast, natural hollow hall as in a cave.

Naked, as if prepared for the entrance of a single person. And whoever entered would be transformed into a "she" or "he." I was the one the room called "she." An I had gone in which the room had given a dimension of she. As if I too were the other side of the cube, the side that goes unseen when looked at straight on.

And in my great dilation, I was in the desert. How can I explain it to you? in the desert as I'd never been before. It was a desert that was calling me as a monotonous and remote canticle calls. I was being seduced. And I was going toward that promising madness. But my fear wasn't that of someone going toward madness, but toward a truth—my fear was of having a truth that I'd come not to want, an infamizing truth that would make me crawl along and be on the roach's level. My first contact with truths always defamed me.

—Hold my hand, because I feel that I'm going. I'm going once again toward the most divine primary life, I'm going toward a hell of raw life. Don't let me see because I'm close to seeing the nucleus of life—and, through the cockroach that even now I'm seeing again, through this specimen of calm living horror, I'm afraid that in this nucleus I'll no longer know what hope is.

The cockroach is pure seduction. Cilia, blinking cilia that keep calling.

I too, who was slowly reducing myself to whatever in me was irreducible, I too had thousands of blinking cilia, and with my cilia I move forward, I protozoan, pure protein. Hold my hand, I reached the irreducible with the inevitability of a death-knell—I sense that all this is ancient and vast, I sense in the hieroglyph of the slow roach the writing of the Far East. And in this desert of great seductions, the creatures: I and the living roach. Life, my love, is a great seduction in which all that exists seduces. That room that was deserted and for that reason primally alive. I had reached the nothing, and the nothing was living and moist.

I HAD REACHED THE NOTHING, AND THE NOTHING was living and moist.

It was then—it was then that as if from a tube the matter began slowly oozing out of the roach that had been crushed.

The roach's matter, which was its insides, the thick, whitish and slow matter, was coming out as from a tube of toothpaste.

Before my nauseated and seduced eyes, the shape of the roach began slowly modifying as it swelled outward. The white matter slowly spilled atop its back like a burden. Immobilized, it was bearing atop its dusty flanks the weight of its own body.

"Scream," I calmly ordered myself. "Scream," I repeated uselessly with a sigh of deep quietude.

The white thickness had halted atop its scales. I looked at the ceiling, briefly resting the eyes that I felt had become deep and large.

But if I screamed even once, I might never again be able to stop. If I screamed nobody could ever help me again; whereas, if I never revealed my neediness, I wouldn't scare anybody and they would help me unawares; but only if I didn't scare anybody by venturing outside the rules. But if they find out, they'll be scared, we who keep the scream as an inviolable secret. If I raised the alarm at being alive, voiceless and hard they would drag me away since they drag away those who depart the possible world, the exceptional being is dragged away, the screaming being.

I looked at the ceiling with heavy eyes. Everything could be fiercely summed up in never emitting a first scream—a first scream unleashes all the others, the first scream at birth unleashes a life, if I screamed I would awaken thousands of screaming beings who would loose upon the rooftops a chorus of screams and horror. If I screamed I would unleash the existence—the existence of what? the existence of the world. With reverence I feared the existence of the world for me.

—Because, hand that sustains me, because I, in a trial I never want again, in a trial for which I ask pardon for myself, I was exiting my world and entering the world.

Because I was no longer seeing myself, I was simply seeing. A whole civilization that had sprung up, with the guarantee that what one sees be mixed immediately with what one feels, an entire civilization whose foundation is salvation—so I was in its ruins. The only ones who could depart this civilization were those whose special role is to depart it: a scientist is given leave, a priest is given permission. But not a woman who doesn't even have the guarantees of a title. And I was fleeing, uneasily I was fleeing.

If you knew the solitude of those first steps of mine. It wasn't like the solitude of a person. It was as if I'd already died and was taking the first steps alone into another life. And it was as if that solitude was called glory, and I too knew it was a glory, and was shivering all over in that divine primal glory that I not only didn't understand, but deeply didn't want.

—Because, you see, I knew I was entering the crude and raw glory of nature. Seduced, I was still fighting as best I could against the quicksand that was swallowing me: and each movement I was making toward "no, no!", each movement pushed me inevitably on; not having the strength to fight was my only forgiveness.

I looked around the room where I'd imprisoned myself, and sought an exit, desperately trying to escape, and inside me I had already shrunk so much that my soul was against the wall—not even able to stop, no longer wanting to stop, fascinated by the certainty of the magnet that was drawing me, I shrank into myself up to the wall where I was implanted in the drawing of the woman. I had shrunk into the marrow of my bones, my last refuge. Where, on the wall, I was so naked that I had no shadow.

And the measurements, the measurements were still the same, I could feel they were, I knew I'd never been more than that woman on the wall, I was she. And I was well preserved, a long and fruitful path.

My tension suddenly snapped like a noise interrupted.

And the first true silence began to whisper. Whatever I'd seen that was so calm and vast and foreign in my dark and smiling photographs—whatever that was was outside for the first time and entirely within my reach, incomprehensible but within my reach.

Which was giving me relief as a thirst is relieved, it was relieving me as if my whole life I'd been waiting for a water as necessary for my bristling body as cocaine is for a body that demands it. Finally the body, soaked with silence, was calming down. The relief came from my fitting into the mute drawing in the cave.

Until that moment I hadn't wholly perceived my struggle, that's how buried I was in it. But now, from the silence into which I had finally fallen, I knew I'd struggled, that I had succumbed and surrendered.

And that, now, I really was in the room.

As inside it as a drawing that has been in a cave for three hundred thousand years. And that's how I fit inside myself, that's how I inside myself was engraved upon the wall.

The narrow route passed through the difficult cockroach, and I'd squeezed with disgust through that body of scales and mud. And I'd ended up, I too completely filthy, emerging through the cockroach into my past that was my continuous present and my continuous future—and that today and always is on the wall, and my fifteen million daughters, from then up to myself, were there too. My life was as continuous as death. Life is so continuous that we divide it into stages, and we call one of them death. I had always been in life, and it matters little that it wasn't I properly speaking, not what I'd usually call I. I was always in life.

I, neutral cockroach body, I with a life that at last doesn't escape me because I finally see it outside of myself—I am the roach, I am my leg, I am my hair, I am the section of whitest light on the plaster of the wall—I am every hellish piece of me—life in me is so demanding that if they hacked me up, like a lizard, the pieces would keep trembling and squirming. I am the silence engraved on a wall, and the oldest butterfly flutters and finds me: the same as always. From birth to death is when I call myself human, and shall never actually die.

But that isn't eternity, it's damnation.

How luxurious this silence is. It's built up of centuries. It's a silence of a roach that's looking. The world looks at itself in me.

Everything looks at everything, everything lives the other; in this desert things know things. Things know things so much that that's ... that's what I'll call forgiveness, if I want to save myself in the human world. It's forgiveness itself. Forgiveness is an attribute of living matter.

FORGIVENESS IS AN ATTRIBUTE OF LIVING MATTER.

—You see, my love, see how out of fear I'm already organizing, see how I still can't deal with these primary laboratory elements without immediately wanting to organize hope. Because for now the metamorphosis of me into myself makes no sense. It's a metamorphosis in which I lose everything I had, and what I had was me—I only have what I am. And what am I now? I am: standing in front of a fright. I am: what I saw. I don't understand and I am afraid to understand, the matter of the world frightens me, with its planets and roaches.

I, who used to live on words of charity or pride or anything. But what an abyss between the word and what it was trying to do, what an abyss between the word love and the love that doesn't even have a human meaning—because—because love is living matter. Is love living matter?

What was it that happened to me yesterday? and now? I'm confused, I crossed deserts and deserts, but did I get stuck by some detail? trapped as beneath a rock.

No, wait, wait: with relief I must remember that I left that room yesterday, I left it, I'm free! and still have a chance to recover. If I want to.

But do I?

What I saw is not organizable. But if I really want to, right now, I could still translate what I found out into terms closer to ours, to human terms, and could still let those hours yesterday pass unnoticed. If I still want to I could, within our language, wonder some other way what happened to me.

And, if I put it that way, I can still find an answer that would let me recover. Recovery would be knowing that: G. H. was a woman who lived well, lived well, lived well, lived on the uppermost layer of the sands of the world, and the sands had never caved in beneath her feet: the coordination was such that, as the sands moved, her feet moved along with them, and so everything stayed firm and compact. G. H. lived on the top floor of a superstructure, and, though built in the air, it was a solid building, she herself in the air, as bees weave life in the air. And that had been happening for centuries, with the necessary or occasional changes, and it worked. It worked—at least nothing spoke and nobody spoke, nobody said no; so it worked.

But, precisely this slow accumulation of centuries automatically piling atop each other was what, without anybody noticing, was making the construction in the air very heavy: it was getting saturated with itself: getting more compact, instead of getting more fragile. The accumulation of living in a superstructure was getting increasingly heavy to stay up in the air.

Like a building in which everyone sleeps calmly at night, unaware that the foundations are sagging and that, in an instant unsuggested by the peacefulness, the beams will give way because their cohesive strength is slowly pulling them apart one millimeter per century. And then, when it's least expected—in an instant as repetitively common as lifting a drink to a smiling mouth during a dance—then, yesterday, on a day as full of sunlight as the days at the height of summer, with men working and kitchens giving off smoke and a jackhammer shattering stones and children laughing and a priest trying to stop, but stop what? yesterday, without warning, there was the loud sound of something solid that suddenly crumbles.

In the collapse, tons fell upon tons. And when I, G. H. even on my suitcases, I, one of the people, opened my eyes, I was—not atop debris, for even the debris had already been swallowed by the sands—I was on a calm plain, kilometers and kilometers below what had been a great city. Things had gone back to being what they were.

The world had reclaimed its own reality, and, as after a catastrophe, my civilization had ended: I was nothing more than a historical fact. Everything in me had been reclaimed by the beginning of time and by my own beginning. I had moved onto the first foreground, I was in the silence of the winds and in the age of tin and copper—in the first age of life.

—Listen, faced with the living cockroach, the worst discovery was that the world is not human, and that we are not human.

No, don't get scared! certainly what had saved me until that moment from the sentimentalized life from which I'd been living, is that the inhuman part is the best part of us, it's the thing, the thing-part of us. That's the only reason that, as a false person, I had never before burrowed beneath the sentimental and utilitarian construction: my human feelings were utilitarian, but I hadn't burrowed under because the thing-part, matter of the God, was too powerful and was waiting to reclaim me. The great neutral punishment of general life is that it can suddenly undermine a single life; if it isn't given its own power, then it bursts as a dam bursts—and arrives pure, unadulterated: purely neutral. That was the great danger: when that neutral part of things doesn't sate a personal life, life arrives purely neutral.

But why exactly in me had the first silence suddenly reappeared? As if a calm woman had simply been called and calmly set aside her embroidery on a chair, stood up, and wordlessly—abandoning her life, renouncing embroidery, love and an already-made soul—wordlessly that woman composedly got down on all fours, started to crawl and drag herself along with calm and sparkling eyes: because the earlier life had called her and she went.

But why me? But why not me. If it hadn't been me, I wouldn't know, and since it was me, I knew—that's all. What was it that called me: madness or reality?

Life was taking revenge on me, and its revenge was no more than coming back, nothing more. In every case of madness something came back. The possessed are not possessed by what is coming but by what is coming back. Sometimes life comes back. If everything broke in me as the force passed through, that's not because its function is to break: it just finally needed to come through since it had already become too copious to be contained or diverted—along its way it buried everything. And afterward, as after a flood, floating upon the waters was a wardrobe, a person, a stray window, three suitcases. And that seemed like hell to me, that destruction of layers and layers of human archeology.

Hell, because the world held no more human meaning for me, and man no longer had human meaning for me. And without that humanization and without the sentimentalization of the world—I am terrified.

Without a cry I looked at the roach.

Seen up close, a roach is an object of great luxury. A bride in black jewels. It is rare, it seems to be one-of-a-kind. In trapping it halfway down its body with the wardrobe door, I had isolated the only known specimen. Only half of its body was visible. The rest, which couldn't be seen, could be huge, and was divided among thousands of houses, behind things and wardrobes. Yet I didn't want the part allotted me. Behind the surface of houses—those murky jewels crawling along?

I was feeling unclean as the Bible speaks of the unclean. Why was the Bible so concerned with the unclean, and made a list of unclean and forbidden animals? why, if those animals, just like the rest, had been created too? And why was the unclean forbidden? I had committed the forbidden act of touching the unclean.

I HAD COMMITTED THE FORBIDDEN ACT OF TOUCHING
the unclean.

And so unclean was I, in that my sudden indirect knowledge of myself, that I opened my mouth to ask for help. They say everything, in the Bible, they say everything—but if I understand what they say, they themselves will call me mad. People just like me have said it, yet to understand them would be my downfall.

"But thou shalt not eat of the impure: which are the eagle, and the griffin, and the falcon." And neither the owl, nor the swan, nor the bat, nor the stork, and any kind of raven.

I was finding out that the unclean animal of the Bible is forbidden because the unclean is the root—for there are created things that never decorated themselves, and preserved themselves exactly as they were the moment they were created, and only they continued to be the still wholly complete root. And because they are the root one cannot eat them, the fruit of good and of evil—eating the living matter would banish me from a paradise of adornments, and leave me to wander forever with a shepherd's staff in the desert. Many were they who wandered with a staff in the desert.

Worse—it would lead me to see that the desert too is alive and has moistness, and to see that everything is alive and made of the same.

To build a possible soul—a soul whose head does not devour its own tail—the law commands us to keep only to what is disguisedly alive. And the law commands that, whoever eats of the unclean, must do so unawares. Since whoever eats of the unclean knowing that it is unclean—will also know that the unclean is not unclean. Is that it?

"And everything that crawls and has wings shall be impure, and not be eaten."

I opened my mouth astonished: it was to ask for a help. Why? why didn't I want to become as unclean as the roach? what ideal was fastening me to the sentiment of an idea? why shouldn't I become unclean, exactly as I was discovering my whole self to be? What was I afraid of? becoming unclean with what?

Becoming unclean with joy.

Since now I understand that what I'd begun to feel was already joy, which I still hadn't recognized or understood. In my mute plea for help, what I was struggling against was a vague first joy that I didn't want to perceive in myself because, even vague, it was already horrible: it was a joy without redemption, I don't know how to explain it to you, but it was a joy without the hope.

—Ah, don't take your hand from mine, I promise myself that perhaps by the end of this impossible story I'll perhaps understand, oh, perhaps on the path of hell I'll come to find what we need—but don't take away your hand, even though I already know that finding has to be along the path of whatever we are, if I manage not to sink definitively into whatever we are.

See, my love, I'm already losing the courage to find whatever I'll have to find, I'm losing the courage to hand myself over to the path and I'm already promising us that in that hell I'll find hope.

—Perhaps it's not the old hope. Perhaps it can't even be called hope.

I was struggling because I didn't want an unknown joy. It would be as forbidden for my future salvation as the forbidden creature that was called unclean—and I was opening and closing my mouth in torture to ask for help, since then it hadn't occurred to me to invent this hand I now invented to hold my own. In my fear yesterday I was alone, and I wanted to ask for help against my first dehumanization.

Dehumanization is as painful as losing everything, as losing everything, my love. I was opening and closing my mouth to ask for help but I couldn't and didn't know how to articulate it.

Because I had nothing more to articulate. My agony was like wanting to speak before dying. I knew I was forever bidding farewell to something, something was going to die, and I wanted to articulate the word that at least summed up whatever was dying.

I finally managed to at least articulate a thought: "I'm asking for help."

It occurred to me then that I didn't have anything to ask for help against. I had nothing to ask.

Suddenly that was it. I was understanding that "asking" was still the last remains of an appealable world that, more and more, was becoming remote. And if I kept wanting to ask it was in order to still cling to the last remains of my old civilization, to cling on so as not to let myself be dragged off by whatever was now demanding me. And to which—in a pleasure without hope—I was already giving in, ah, I already wanted to give in—to have experienced it was already the beginning of a hell of wanting, wanting, wanting.... Was my will to want stronger than my will for salvation?

More and more I had nothing to ask for. And I was seeing, with fascination and horror, the pieces of my rotten mummy clothes falling dry to the floor, I was watching my transformation from chrysalis into moist larva, my wings were slowly shrinking back scorched. And a belly entirely new and made for the ground, a new belly was being reborn.

Without taking my eyes off the cockroach, I began lowering myself until I felt my body meeting the bed and, without taking my eyes from the cockroach, I sat.

Now it was with raised eyes that I was seeing it. Now, bent over its own midriff, it was looking down at me. I had fastened before me the unclean of the world—and had broken the spell of the living thing. I had lost the ideas.

Then, once again, another thick millimeter of white matter spurted out.

THEN, ONCE AGAIN, ANOTHER THICK MILLIMETER OF white matter spurted out.

Holy Mary, mother of God, I offer thee my life in exchange for that moment yesterday's not being true. The roach with the white matter was looking at me. I don't know if it was seeing me, I don't know what a roach sees. But we were looking at each other, and also I don't know what a woman sees. But if its eyes weren't seeing me, its existence was existing me—in the primary world I had entered, beings exist others as a way of seeing one another. And in that world I was coming to know, there are several ways that mean seeing: one a looking at the other without seeing him, one possessing the other, one eating the other, one just being in a place and the other being there too: all that also means seeing. The roach wasn't seeing me directly, it was with me. The roach wasn't seeing me with its eyes but with its body.

And I—I was seeing. There was no way not to see it. No way to deny: my convictions and my wings were quickly drying up and no longer had a point. I could no longer deny it. I don't

73

know what I could no longer deny, but I no longer could. And I could no longer even rescue myself, as before, with a whole civilization that would help me deny what I was seeing.

I was seeing all of it, the roach.

The roach is an ugly and sparkling being. The roach is the other way around. No, no, it doesn't have a way around: it is that. Whatever is exposed in it is what I hide in me: from my outside being exposed I made my unheeded inside. It was looking at me. And it wasn't a face. It was a mask. A diver's mask. That precious gem of rusted iron. Its two eyes were alive like two ovaries. It was looking at me with the blind fertility of its gaze. It was fertilizing my dead fertility. Would its eyes be salty? If I touched them—since I was gradually getting more and more unclean—if I touched them with my mouth, would they taste salty?

I'd already tasted in my mouth a man's eyes and, from the salt in my mouth, realized he was crying.

But, thinking about the salt in the roach's black eyes, suddenly I recoiled again, and my dry lips pulled back to my teeth: the reptiles that move across the earth! In the halted reverberation of the light of the room, the roach was a small slow crocodile. The dry and vibrating room. The roach and I poised in that dryness as on the dry crust of an extinct volcano. That desert I had entered, and also inside it I was discovering life and its salt.

Once again the white part of the roach spurted out maybe less than a millimeter.

This time I had hardly perceived the minute movement its matter had made. I was looking on engrossed, unmoving.

—Never, until then, had life happened to me by day. Never in sunlight. Only in my nights did the world slowly revolve.

Only that, whatever happened in the dark of night itself, would also happen at the same time in my own entrails, and my dark wasn't differentiated from the dark outside, and in the morning, when I opened my eyes, the world was still a surface: the secret life of the night soon reduced in my mouth to the taste of a nightmare that disappears. But now life was happening by day. Undeniable and to be seen. Unless I averted my eyes.

And I could still avert my eyes.

—But hell had already taken me, my love, the hell of unhealthy curiosity. I was already selling my human soul, because seeing had already begun to consume me in pleasure, I was selling my future, I was selling my salvation, I was selling us.

"I'm asking for help," I then suddenly shouted to myself with the muteness of those whose mouths are gradually filled with quicksand, "I'm asking for help," I thought still and seated. Yet not once did it occur to me to get up and go, as if that were already impossible. The roach and I had been buried in a mine.

The scale just had one pan on it now. Upon that pan was my deep refusal of roaches. But now "refusal of roaches" were merely words, and I also knew that in the hour of my death I too would not be translatable by word.

Dying, yes, I knew, since dying was the future and is imaginable, and for imagining I had always had time. But the instant, this instant—the present—that isn't imaginable, between the present and I there's no interval: it is now, in me.

—Understand, dying I knew beforehand and dying still wasn't demanding me. But what I'd never experienced was the crash with the moment called "right now." Today is demanding me this very day. I had never before known that the time to live also has no word. The time to live, my love, was being so right now that I leaned my mouth on the matter of life. The time to live is a slow uninterrupted creaking of doors continuously opening wide. Two gates were opening and had never stopped opening. But they were continuously opening onto—onto the nothing?

The time to live is so hellishly inexpressive that it is the nothing. What I was calling "nothing" was nevertheless so stuck to me that to me it was … I? and that's why it was becoming invisible as I was invisible to myself, and it was becoming the nothing. The doors as always kept opening.

Finally, my love, I gave in. And it became a now.

FINALLY, MY LOVE, I GAVE IN. AND IT BECAME A NOW.

It was finally now. It was simply now. It was like this: the country was in eleven in the morning. Superficially as a yard that is green, of the most delicate superficiality. Green, green—green is a yard. Between me and the green, the water of the air. The green water of the air. I see everything through a full glass. Nothing is heard. In the rest of the house the shadows are all swollen. The ripe superficiality. It's eleven in the morning in Brazil. It's now. That means exactly now. Now is time swollen to the limit. Eleven o'clock has no depth. Eleven o'clock is full of eleven hours up to the brim of the green glass. Time trembles as a motionless balloon. The air fertilized and wheezing. Until in a national anthem the ringing of eleven-thirty cuts the cables of the balloon. And suddenly we will all reach noon. Which will be green like now.

I suddenly awoke from the unexpected green oasis where for a moment I had taken full refuge.

But I was in the desert. And it isn't only at the summit of an oasis that it's now: now is also in the desert, and fully. It was right now. For the first time in my life it was fully about now. This was the greatest brutality I had ever received.

For the present has no hope, and the present has no future: the future will be exactly once again present.

I was so scared that I got even quieter inside myself. Because it was seeming to me that I would finally have to feel.

It seems I shall have to give up everything I leave behind the gates. And I know, I knew, that if I went through the gates that are always open, I would enter the heart of nature.

I knew that entering is not a sin. But it's risky as dying. Just as one dies without knowing where to, and that is the greatest courage of a body. Entering was only a sin because it was the damnation of my life, to which I later might never be able to regress. I might have already known that, beyond the gates, there would be no difference between me and the roach. Not in my own eyes or in the eyes of what is God.

That was how I started taking my first steps into the nothing. My first hesitant steps toward Life, and abandoning my life. My foot stepped into the air, and I entered paradise or hell: the nucleus.

I ran my hand over my forehead: with relief I was noticing that I had finally begun to sweat. Shortly before there was just that hot dryness scorching us both. Now I was beginning to moisten myself.

Ah, how tired I am. My desire now would be to interrupt all of this and insert in this difficult story, purely for the sake of fun and relaxation, a great anecdote I heard the other day about why a couple broke up. Ah, I know so many interesting stories. And I could also, to relax, speak of tragedy. I know tragedies.

My sweat was relieving me. I looked up, at the ceiling. With the play of the beams of light, the ceiling had rounded and transformed itself into something that reminded me of a vault. The vibration of the heat was like the vibration of a sung oratorio. Only my hearing part was feeling. Closed-mouth canticle, sound vibrating deaf like something imprisoned and contained, amen, amen. Canticle of thanksgiving for the murder of one being by another being.

The deepest murder: the one that is a way of relating, a way of one being existing the other being, a way of seeing one other and being one other and having one other, murder where there is neither victim nor executioner, but a link of mutual ferocity. My primary struggle for life. "Lost in the Fiery Hell of a Canyon a Woman Desperately Struggles for Life."

I waited for that mute and imprisoned sound to pass. But the vastness inside the little room was growing, the mute oratorio was enlarging it in vibrations that reached the fissure in the ceiling. The oratorio was not a prayer: it was not asking for anything. Passions in the form of an oratorio.

The roach suddenly vomited through its slit another fluffy and white spurt.

—Ah! but who can I ask for help, if you too—I then thought toward a man who had been mine—if you aren't any use to me now either. Since like me, you wanted to transcend life and therefore surpassed it. But now I won't be able to transcend anymore, I will have to know, and will go without you, whom I tried to ask for help. Pray for me, my mother, since not transcending is a sacrifice, and transcending used to be my human effort at salvation, there was an immediate usefulness in transcending. Transcending is a transgression. But staying inside whatever is, that demands that I be fearless!

And I will have to stay inside whatever is.

There's something that must be said, don't you feel that

there's something that must be known? oh, even if I have to transcend it later, even if later the transcending is born inescapably from me like the breath of someone alive.

But, after what I found out, I'll accept like a breath of respiration—or like a noxious vapor? no, not like a noxious vapor, I take pity on me! if the transcendence must come to me inescapably, may it be like the breath born of the mouth itself, of the mouth that exists, and not of a false mouth open on the arm or head.

It was with hellish joy that I as if I were going to die. I was starting to feel that my haunted step would be irremediable, and that I was little by little abandoning my human salvation. I was feeling that what is mine inside me, despite its fluffy and white matter, nevertheless had the power to explode my face of silver and beauty, farewell beauty of the world. Beauty that now is remote to me and that I no longer want—I am no longer able to want beauty—maybe I never had really wanted it, but it was so good! and I remember how the game of beauty was good, beauty was a continuous transmutation.

But with hellish relief I bid it farewell. What comes out of the roach's belly is not transcendable—ah, I don't want to say that it's the opposite of beauty, "opposite of beauty" doesn't even make sense—what comes out of the roach is: "today," blessed be the fruit of thy womb—I want the present without dressing it up with a future that redeems it, not even with a hope—until now what hope wanted in me was just to conjure away the present.

But I want much more than that: I want to find the redemption in today, in right now, in the reality that is being, and not in the promise, I want to find joy in this instant—I want the God in whatever comes out of the roach's belly—even if that, in my former human terms, means the worst, and, in human terms, the infernal.

Yes, I wanted it. But at the same time I was grabbing with both hands onto the pit of my stomach: "I can't!" I implored of another man who also could not and never could. I can't! I don't want to know what the thing I would now call "the nothing" is made of! I don't want to feel directly in my very delicate mouth the salt in the eyes of the roach, because, my mother, I had been used to the sogginess of its layers and not the simple moistness of the thing.

It was as I was thinking about the salt in the roach's eyes that, with the sigh of someone who is going to have to give in yet again, I realized that I was still using the old human beauty: salt.

Even the beauty of salt and the beauty of tears I would have to abandon. Even that, since what I was seeing predated humanity.

SINCE WHAT I WAS SEEING PREDATED HUMANITY.

No, there was no salt in those eyes. I was sure that the roach's eyes were saltless. For salt I had always been ready, salt was the transcendence that I used to experience a taste, and to flee what I was calling "nothing." For salt I was ready, for salt I had built my entire self. But what my mouth wouldn't know how to understand—was the saltless. What all of me didn't know—was the neutral.

And the neutral was the life that I used to call the nothing. The neutral was the hell.

The Sun had moved a bit and stuck itself to my back. Also in the sunlight the roach was split in two. I can't do anything for you, roach. I don't want to do anything for you.

Because it was no longer about doing something: the neutral gaze of the roach was telling me it wasn't about that, and I knew it. Only I couldn't bear just sitting there and being, and so I wanted to do. Doing would be transcending, transcending is an exit.

But the moment had come for it no longer to be about that. Since the roach didn't know about hope or pity. If it weren't imprisoned and were larger than I, with neutral busy pleasure it would kill me. Just as the violent neutral of its life was allowing me, because I was not imprisoned and was larger, to kill it. That was the kind of tranquil neutral ferocity of the desert where we were.

And its eyes were saltless, not salty as I would have wanted: salt would be the feeling and the word and the taste. I knew that the neutral of the roach has the same lack of taste as its white matter. Seated, I was consisting. Seated, consisting, I was realizing that if I didn't call things salty or sweet, sad or happy or painful or even with in-between shades of greater subtlety—that only then would I no longer be transcending and remain in the thing itself.

That thing, whose name I do not know, was that thing that, looking at the roach, I was now starting to call without a name. Contact with that thing without qualities or attributes was disgusting to me, a living thing with no name, or taste, or smell was repugnant. Insipidity: the taste now was no more than a tartness: my own tartness. For a moment, then, I felt a kind of quaking happiness all over my body, a horrible happy unease in which my legs seemed to vanish, as always when the roots of my unknown identity were touched.

Ah, at least I had already entered the roach's nature to the point that I no longer wanted to do anything for it. I was freeing myself from my morality, and that was a catastrophe without crash and without tragedy.

Morality. Would it be simplistic to think the moral problem with regard to others consists in behaving as one ought to, and the moral problem with regards to oneself is managing to feel what one ought to? Am I moral to the extent that I do what I should, and feel as I should? All of a sudden the moral question seemed to me not only overwhelming, but extremely petty. The moral problem, in order for us to adjust to it, should be at once less demanding and greater. Since as an ideal it is both small and unattainable. Small, if one attains it: unattainable, because it cannot even be attained. "The scandal still is necessary, but woe to him through whom the scandal comes"—was it in the New Testament that it was said? The solution had to be secret. The ethics of the moral is keeping it secret. Freedom is a secret.

Though I know that, even in secret, freedom doesn't take care of guilt. But one must be greater than guilt. The tiny divine part of me is greater than my human guilt. The God is greater than my essential guilt. So I prefer the God, to my guilt. Not to excuse myself and to flee but because guilt diminishes me.

I no longer wanted to do anything for the roach. I was freeing myself from my morality—though that gave me fear, curiosity and fascination; and much fear. I'm not going to do anything for you, I too creep along the ground. I'm not going to do anything for you because I no longer know the meaning of love as I used to think I did. Also what I thought about love, that too I'm bidding farewell, I barely know what it is anymore, I don't remember.

Maybe I'll find another name, much crueler initially, and much more it-self. Or maybe I won't. Is love when you don't give a name to the identity of things?

But now I know something horrible: I know what it is to need, need, need. And it's a new need, on a level that I can only call neutral and terrible. It's a need without any pity on my need and without pity on the roach's need. I was seated, calm, sweating, exactly as now—and I see that there is something more serious and more inevitable and more nucleus than everything I used to call by names. I, who called love my hope for love.

But now, it's in this neutral present of nature and of the roach and of the living sleep of my body, that I want to know love. And I want to know if hope was a contemporization with the impossible. Or if it was a way of delaying what's possible now—and which I only don't have out of fear. I want the present time that has no promise, that is, that is being. This is the core of what I want and fear. This is the nucleus that I never wanted.

The roach was touching all of me with its black, faceted, shiny and neutral gaze.

And now I was starting to let it touch me. In truth I had fought all my life against the profound desire to let myself be touched—and I had fought because I couldn't allow myself the death of what I called my goodness; the death of human goodness. But now I no longer wanted to fight it. There had to be a goodness so other that it wouldn't resemble goodness. I no longer wanted to fight.

With disgust, with despair, with courage, I was giving in. It was too late, and now I wanted.

Was it only in that instant that I was wanting? No, or else I would have left the room long before, or simply would barely have seen the roach—how often before had roaches happened to me and I had gone another way? I was giving in, but with fear and shattering.

I thought that if the telephone rang, I would have to answer and would still be saved! But, as if remembering an extinct world, I remembered that I'd taken the phone off the hook. If not for that, it would ring, I would flee the room to answer it, and never again, oh! never again would return.

—I remembered you, when I kissed your man face, slowly, slowly kissed it, and when the time came to kiss your eyes—I remembered that then I had tasted the salt in my mouth, and that the salt of tears in your eyes was my love for you. But, what bound me most of all in a fright of love, had been, in the depth of the depths of the salt, your saltless and innocent and childish substance: with my kiss your deepest insipid life was given to me, and kissing your face was the saltless and busy patient work of love, it was woman weaving a man, just as you had woven me, neutral crafting of life.

NEUTRAL CRAFTING OF LIFE.

Through having one day kissed the insipid residue found in the salt of a tear, the unfamiliarity of the room became recognizable, like matter already lived. If it hadn't been recognized until then, it was because it had only been saltlessly lived by my deepest saltless blood. I was recognizing the familiarity of everything. The figures on the wall, I was recognizing them with a new way of looking. And I was also recognizing the roach's watchfulness. The roach's watchfulness was life living, my own watchful life living itself.

I felt around in the pockets of my robe, found a cigarette and matches, lit it.

In the sun the white mass of the roach was becoming drier and slightly yellowed. That informed me that more time had passed than I'd imagined. A cloud covered the sun for an instant, and suddenly I was seeing the same room without sun.

Not dark but just without light. So I noticed that the room existed by itself, that it wasn't the heat of the sun, it could also be cold and calm as the moon. Imagining its possible moonlit night, I breathed in deeply as if entering a quiet reservoir.

Though I also knew that the cold moon wouldn't be the room either. The room was in itself. It was the loud monotony of an eternity that breathes. That terrified me. The world would only cease to terrify me if I became the world. If I were the world, I wouldn't be afraid. If we are the world, we are moved by a delicate radar that guides.

When the cloud passed, the sun in the room became even brighter and whiter.

From time to time, for a light instant, the roach moved its antennae. Its eyes kept looking at me monotonously, the two neutral and fertile ovaries. In them I was recognizing my two anonymous neutral ovaries. And I didn't want to, ah, how I didn't want to!

I'd taken the phone off the hook, but somebody could maybe ring the doorbell, and I'd be free! The blouse! that I'd bought, they'd said they'd deliver it, and then they'd ring the bell!

No, they wouldn't. I'd have to keep recognizing. And I was recognizing in the roach the saltlessness of the time I was pregnant.

—I recalled myself roaming the streets knowing I'd have the abortion, doctor, I who about children only knew and only would know that I was going to have an abortion. But at least I was getting to know pregnancy. Along the streets I was feeling inside me the child that still wasn't moving, while I was stopping to look in the shop windows at the smiling wax mannequins. And when I entered a restaurant and ate, the pores of a child were devouring like the mouth of a waiting fish. When I was walking, when I was walking I was carrying it.

During the interminable hours that I roamed the streets making up my mind about the abortion, which I had nevertheless already arranged with you, sir, doctor, during those hours my eyes too must have been saltless. On the street I too was no more than thousands of cilia of a neutral protozoan beating, I had already known within myself the shiny gaze of a roach captured at the waist. I had walked the streets with my lips parched, and living, doctor, was for me the opposite side of a crime. Pregnancy: I had been flung into the happy horror of the neutral life that lives and moves.

And while I was looking at the shop windows, doctor, with my lips as parched as someone who doesn't breathe through her nose, while I was looking at the fixed and smiling mannequins, I was full of neutral plankton, and was opening my suffocated and quiet mouth, I said this to you, sir: "what's bothering me most, doctor, is that I'm having trouble breathing." The plankton was giving me my color, the Tapajós River is green because its plankton is green.

When night arrived, I was making up my mind about the abortion I'd already made up my mind about, lying on the bed with my thousands of faceted eyes spying on the dark, with lips blackened from breathing, without thinking, without thinking, making up my mind, making up my mind: on those nights all of me was slowly blackening from my own plankton just as the matter of the roach was yellowing, and my gradual blackening was keeping track of the passing time. And was all that love for the child?

If so, then love is much more than love: love is something before love: it's plankton struggling, and the great living neutrality struggling. Just like the life in the roach stuck at the waist.

The fear I always had of the silence with which life makes itself. Fear of the neutral. The neutral was my deepest and most living root—I looked at the roach and knew. Until the moment of seeing the roach I'd always had some name for what I was living, otherwise I wouldn't get away. To escape the neutral, I had long since forsaken the being for the persona, for the human mask. When I humanized myself, I'd freed myself from the desert.

I'd freed myself from the desert, yes, but had also lost it! and also lost the forests, and lost the air, and lost the embryo inside me.

But there it is, the neutral roach, without a name for pain or for love. Its only differentiation in life is that it has to be either male or female. I had only thought of it as female, since things crushed at the waist are female.

I put out the cigarette butt that was already burning my fingers, I put it out carefully on the floor with my slipper, and crossed my sweaty legs, I had never thought legs could sweat that much. The two of us, the ones buried alive. If I had the courage, and I'd wipe the sweat from the roach.

Did it feel inside itself something like what my gaze saw in it? how much did it take advantage of itself and take advantage of what it was? even somehow indirectly, did it know that it crawled? or is crawling something we ourselves don't know is happening? What did I know about whatever it was that others obviously saw in me? how would I know if I went around with my stomach pressed into the dust of the ground. Truth has no witness? being isn't knowing? If a person doesn't look and doesn't see, does the truth exist anyway? The truth that doesn't transmit itself even to those who can see. Is that the secret of being a person?

If I wanted to, even now, after everything that's happened, I can still keep myself from having seen. And then I'll never know about the truth I'm trying again to cross—it still depends on me!

I was looking around the dry and white room, from which I could only see sands and sands of wreckage, some covering others. The minaret where I was standing was made of hard gold. I was upon the hard gold that receives nothing. And I was needing to be received. I was afraid.

—Mother: I killed a life, and there are no arms to receive me now and in the hour of our desert, amen. Mother, everything now has turned to hard gold. I interrupted an organized thing, mother, and that is worse than killing, that made me enter through a breach that showed me, worse than death, that showed me the thick and neutral life turning yellow. The roach is alive, its eye gaze is fertilizing, I am afraid of my hoarseness, mother.

Because my mute hoarseness was already the hoarseness of someone enjoying a gentle hell.

The hoarseness—of someone having pleasure. The hell was good for me, I was enjoying that white blood that I had spilled. The roach is real, mother. It is no longer an idea of a roach.

—Mother, all I did was want to kill, but just look at what I broke: I broke a casing! Killing is also forbidden because it breaks the hard casing, and leaves one with the sticky life. From inside the hard casing is emerging a heart thick and white and alive with pus, mother, blessed art thou among the roaches, now and in the hour of this thy my death, cockroach and jewel.

As if having said the word "mother" had freed inside myself a thick and white part—the intense vibration of the oratorio suddenly stopped, and the minaret fell mute. And as after an intense attack of vomiting, my forehead was relieved, fresh and cold. No longer even fear, no longer even fright.

NO LONGER EVEN FEAR, NO LONGER EVEN FRIGHT.

Had I vomited my last human remnants? And I was no longer asking for help. The diurnal desert was before me. And now the oratorio was starting up again but in another way, now the oratorio was the deaf sound of the heat refracting off walls and ceilings, in rounded vaults. The oratorio was made of the tremblings of sultriness. And my fear too was different now: not the fear of someone about to enter, but the much broader fear of someone who has already entered.

So much broader: it was fear of my lack of fear.

Since it was with my rashness that I then looked at the roach. And I saw: it was a creature without beauty for other species. And as I saw it, the little former fear returned for just an instant: "I swear, I'll do everything you want! but don't leave me imprisoned in the roach's room because something enormous is going to happen to me, I don't want the other species! I just want people."

But, at my slight cringing, the oratorio just intensified, and so I kept still, no longer trying to make a movement to help myself. I'd already abandoned myself—I could nearly see there at the beginning of the path already traveled the body I'd cast off. But I was still sometimes calling for it, still calling myself. And it was because I could no longer hear my answer, that I knew I'd already abandoned myself beyond my reach.

Yes, the roach was a creature without beauty for other species. The mouth: if it had teeth, they would be big, square and yellow teeth. How I hate the light of the sun that reveals everything, reveals even the possible. With the edge of my robe I wiped my forehead, without taking my gaze from the roach's eyes, and my own eyes also had the same lashes as well. But no one touches yours, unclean thing. Only another roach would want this roach.

And me—who would want me today? who had already become as mute as I was? who, like me, was calling fear love? and want, love? and need, love? Who, like me, knew that I had never changed my form since they had drawn me on the stone of a cave? and next to a man and a dog.

From now on I could call anything by the name I invented: in the dry room I could, since any name would do, since none of them would. Within the dry sounds of the vault everything could be called anything, because anything would be transmuted in the same vibrating muteness. The roach's much greater nature made anything, entering there—name or person—lose its false transcendence. So much so that I was seeing only and exactly the white vomit of its body: I was only seeing facts and things. I knew that I was in the irreducible, though I was unaware what the irreducible is.

But I also knew that ignorance of the law of the irreducible was no excuse. I could no longer excuse myself by claiming I didn't know the law—since knowing oneself and knowing the world is the law that, even unattainable, cannot be infringed, and nobody can be excused by claiming not to know it. Worse: the roach and I were not faced with a law we had to obey: we ourselves were the unknown law that we obeyed. The renewedly original sin is this: I must fulfill my law of which I am unaware, and if I don't fulfill my ignorance, I shall be originally sinning against life.

In the garden of Paradise, who was the monster and who was not? between the houses and apartments, and in the elevated spaces between the high buildings, in that hanging garden—who is, and who is not? How long can I stand not at least knowing what is looking at me? the raw roach is looking at me, and its law sees mine. I felt that I was going to know.

—Don't abandon me now, don't let me make alone this already-made decision. I had, yes, I still had the desire to take refuge in my own fragility and in the sly, yet true, argument that my shoulders were a woman's, feeble and slender. Whenever I had needed to, I'd excused myself by arguing that I was a woman. But I was well aware that it's not just women who are afraid to see, everyone fears seeing what is God.

I was afraid of the face of God, I was afraid of my final nudity on the wall. Beauty, that new absence of beauty that had nothing to do with whatever I used to call beauty, horrified me.

—Give me your hand. Because I no longer know what I'm saying. I think I made it all up, none of this existed! But if I made up what happened to me yesterday—who can guarantee that I didn't also invent my entire life prior to yesterday?

Give me your hand:

GIVE ME YOUR HAND:

I am now going to tell you how I entered the inexpressive that was always my blind and secret search. How I entered whatever exists between the number one and the number two, how I saw the line of mystery and fire, and which is surreptitious line. A note exists between two notes of music, between two facts exists a fact, between two grains of sand no matter how close together there exists an interval of space, a sense that exists between senses—in the interstices of primordial matter is the line of mystery and fire that is the breathing of the world, and the continual breathing of the world is what we hear and call silence.

It wasn't by using any of my attributes as an instrument that I was reaching the smooth mysterious fire of whatever is a plasma—it was precisely removing from myself all my attributes, and going only with my living entrails. To have reached that point, I was abandoning my human organization—to enter that monstrous thing that is my living neutrality.

—I know, it's bad to hold my hand. It's bad to be left without air in that collapsed mine where I brought you without

99

mercy on you, but out of mercy on me. But I swear I'll get you out of here still alive—even though I'm not lying, even though I'm not lying about what my eyes saw. I'll save you from this terror in which, for the time being, I need you. What mercy on you now, you whom I grabbed. You innocently gave me your hand, and because I was holding it I had the courage to submerge myself. But don't try to understand me, just keep me company. I know your hand would drop me, if it knew.

How can I repay you? At least use me too, use me at least like a dark tunnel—and when you've crossed my darkness you'll find yourself on the other side with yourself. You might not find yourself with me, I don't know if I'll cross over, but with yourself. At least you're not alone, as I was yesterday, and yesterday I was only praying to at least get out of there alive. And not just alive—the way that primarily monstrous roach was just alive—but organizedly alive like a person.

Identity—identity that is the first inherence—was that what I was surrendering to? was that what I had entered?

Identity is forbidden to me, I know. But I'm going to take a chance because I trust in my future cowardice, and it will be my essential cowardice that will reorganize me once again into a person.

Not only through my cowardice. But I'll reorganize myself through the ritual with which I was already born, as in the neutral of the semen the ritual of life is inherent. Identity is forbidden to me but my love is so great that I won't resist my will to enter the mysterious fabric, into that plasma from which I may never again be able to depart. My belief, however, is also so deep that, if I cannot depart, I know, even in my new unreality the plasma of the God will be in my life.

Ah, but at the same time how can I want for my heart to see? if my body is so weak that I can't face the sun without my eyes physically crying—how could I stop my heart from glittering in physically organic tears if in nakedness I felt the identity: the God? My heart that covered itself with a thousand cloaks.

The great neutral reality of what I was living was overtaking me with its extreme objectivity. I was feeling incapable of being as real as the reality that was reaching me—could I be commencing in contortions to be as nakedly real as what I was seeing? Yet I was living all that reality with a feeling of the unreality of reality. Could I be living, not the truth, but the myth of the truth? Every time I lived the truth it was through an impression of inescapable dream: the inescapable dream is my truth.

I'm trying to tell you how I reached the neutral and the inexpressive in me. I don't know if I'm understanding what I'm saying, I'm feeling—and I very much fear the feeling, since feeling is only one of the types of being. Yet I shall cross the stupefied sultriness that billows from the nothing, and shall have to understand the neutral with the feeling.

The neutral. I am speaking of the vital element that binds things. Oh, I am not afraid that you don't understand, but that I understand myself badly. If I don't understand myself, I'll die from the same thing I live from. Now let me tell you the scariest part:

I was being carried off by the demonic.

For the inexpressive is diabolic. A person who isn't committed to hope lives the demonic. A person who has the courage to cast off feelings discovers the ample life of an extremely busy silence, the same that exists in the cockroach, the same in the stars, the same in the self—the demonic *precedes* the human. And the person who sees that presentness burns as if seeing the God. Prehuman divine life is of a presentness that burns.

PREHUMAN DIVINE LIFE IS OF A PRESENTNESS THAT burns.

I'm going to tell you: I feared a certain blind and already ferocious joy that was starting to overtake me. And to lose me.

The joy of getting lost is a Sabbath joy. Getting lost is a dangerous finding. I was experiencing in that desert the fire of things: and it was a neutral fire. I was living from the tessitura of which things are made. And it was a hell, that place, because in that world where I was living neither compassion nor hope exists.

I had entered the Sabbath orgy. Now I know what happens in the dark of the mountains on the nights of orgies. I know! I know with horror: things enjoy themselves. The thing of which things are made delights itself—that is the raw joy of black magic. It was from that neutral that I lived—the neutral was my true primeval soup. I was moving forward, and feeling the joy of the hell.

And the hell is not the torture of pain! it is the torture of a joy.

The neutral is inexplicable and alive, try to understand me: just as protoplasm and semen and protein are of a living neutral. And I was all new, like a novice. It was as if before I had had a palate addicted to salt and sugar, and a soul addicted to joys and pains—and had never felt the first taste. And now I was experiencing the taste of the nothing. I was rapidly becoming unaddicted, and the taste was new as the mother's milk that only has taste for an infant's mouth. With the landslide of my civilization and of my humanity—which was a suffering of great longing for me—with the loss of humanity, I was coming orgiastically to taste the identity of things.

It's very difficult to taste. Up till then I had been so engrossed by sentimentalization that, experiencing the taste of the real identity, it seemed as tasteless as the taste a raindrop has in your mouth. It's horribly insipid, my love.

My love, it's like the most insipid nectar—it's like the air that in itself has no smell. Up till then my addicted senses were mute to the taste of things. But the most archaic and demonic of my thirsts had led me subterraneously to collapse all constructions. The sinful thirst was guiding me—and now I know that experiencing the taste of that almost nothing is the secret joy of the gods. It is a nothing that is the God—and that has no taste.

But it's the most primary joy. And only that, at last, at last! is the pole opposite the pole of the feeling-human-Christian. Through the pole of the primary demonic joy, I was remotely perceiving and for the first time—that there really was an opposite pole.

I was clean of my own intoxification by feeling, so clean I could enter the divine life that was a primary life entirely without comeliness, life as primary as if it were a manna falling from heaven and that doesn't have the taste of anything:

manna is like a rain and has no taste. Experiencing that taste of the nothing was my damnation and my joyful terror.

Oh, my unknown love, remember that I was imprisoned there in the collapsed mine, and that by then the room had taken on an unutterable familiarity, like the truthful familiarity of dreams. And, as in dreams, what I can't reproduce for you is the essential color of its atmosphere. As in dreams, the "logic" was something else, was one that makes no sense when you awaken, since the dream's greater truth is lost.

But remember that all this was happening with me awake and immobilized by the light of day, and the truth of a dream was happening without the anesthesia of the night. Sleep with me awake, and only thus can you know of my great sleep and know what is the living desert.

Suddenly, sitting there, a tiredness all hardened and without any lassitude, overtook me. A little more and it would petrify me.

Then, carefully, as if I already had paralyzed parts within me, I started stretching out on the coarse mattress and there, all shriveled up, I fell asleep as immediately as a roach falls asleep on a vertical wall. There was no human stability in my sleep: it was the balancing power of a roach that falls asleep atop the lime of a wall.

When I woke, the room had a sun even whiter and more fervidly motionless. Returning from that sleep, to whose depthless surface my short paws had clung, I was now trembling with cold.

But then the numbness was passing, and once again, fully inside the burning of the sun, I was suffocating confined.

It must have been past noon. I got up before even making up my mind to, and, though uselessly, tried to open even more the already wide open window, and was trying to breathe, even if only to breathe a visual expanse, I was seeking an expanse.

I WAS SEEKING AN EXPANSE.

From that room excavated in the rock of a building, from the window of my minaret, I saw as far as the eye could see the enormous range of roofs and roofs calmly scorching in the sun. The apartment buildings like squat villages. In size it surpassed Spain.

Beyond the rocky gullies, between the cements of the buildings, I saw the favela atop the hill and saw a goat slowly climbing the hill. Beyond stretched the highlands of Asia Minor. From there I was contemplating the empire of the present. Over there was the Strait of the Dardanelles. Further beyond the craggy ridges. Thy majestic monotony. Under the sun thy imperial breadth.

And further beyond, already the start of the sands. The desert naked and burning. When darkness fell, cold would consume the desert, and in it one would shiver as on desert nights. Even further, the blue and salty lake was sparkling. Over there, that must be the region of the great salt lakes.

Beneath the trembling waves of sultriness, monotony.

Through the other apartment windows and on the cement terraces, I was seeing a coming and going of shadows and people, like those of the first Assyrian merchants. They were fighting for control of Asia Minor.

I had dug up the future perhaps—or reached such remote ancient depths that my hands that had dug them up could not fathom them. There I was standing, like a child dressed as a friar, a sleepy child. But an inquisitive child. From atop this building, the present contemplates the present. Just as in the second millennium before Christ.

And I, now I was no longer an inquisitive child. I had grown, and had become as simple as a queen. Kings, sphinxes and lions—here is the city where I live, and all extinct. I was what was left, stuck by one of the stones that had fallen. And, since the silence judged my immobility to be that of a dead woman, they all forgot me, they left without pulling me out, and, presumed dead, I lay there watching. And I saw, while the silence of those who really had died was invading me as ivy invades the mouths of the stone lions.

And because I myself was then sure I would end up dying of starvation beneath the fallen stone that was pinning me by my limbs—I then saw like someone who is never going to tell. I saw, as uninvolved as someone who isn't even going to tell herself. I was seeing, like someone who will never have to understand what she saw. As a lizard's nature sees: without even having to remember afterward. The lizard sees—as a loose eye sees.

I was perhaps the first person to set foot in that castle in the air. Five million years ago perhaps the last caveman had looked out from this same point, where once there must have existed a mountain. And that later, eroded, had become an empty area where later once again cities had risen which themselves in turn eroded. Today the ground is widely populated by diverse races.

Standing at the window, sometimes my eyes rested on the blue lake that might have been no more than a piece of sky. But I soon grew tired, since the blue was made of much intensity of light. My bleary eyes then went to rest in the naked and burning desert, which at least didn't have the hardness of a color. Three millennia later the secret oil would gush from those sands: the present was opening gigantic perspectives onto a new present.

Meanwhile, today, I was living in the silence of something that three millennia later, after it was eroded and built again, would be stairs again, cranes, men and constructions. I was living the pre-history of a future. Like a woman who never had children but would have them three millennia later, I was already living today from the oil that would gush in three millennia.

If at least I'd entered the room at dusk—tonight the moon would be full, I remembered when recalling the party on the terrace the night before—I would see the full moon rising over the desert.

"Ah, I want to go back to my house," I suddenly asked myself, since the moist moon had made me long for my life. But from that platform I couldn't manage a single moment of darkness and moon. Only the heap of embers, only the errant wind. And for me no flask of water, no vessel of food.

But maybe, less than a year later, I'd make a find that nobody and not even me would have dared to expect. A gold chalice?

For I was seeking the treasure of my city.

A city of gold and stone, Rio de Janeiro, whose inhabitants under the sun were six hundred thousand beggars. The treasure of the city could be in one of the breaches in the rubble.

But which one? That city needed the work of a cartographer.

Raising my gaze ever further, to ever steeper heights, before me lay gigantic blocks of buildings that formed a heavy design, still not shown on a map. My eyes went on, seeking on the hill the remains of some fortified wall. Reaching the top of the hill, I let my eyes circumnavigate the panorama. Mentally I traced a circle around the semi-ruins of the favelas, and recognized that there once could have been a city living there as large and limpid as Athens at its apogee, with children running between the merchandise displayed in the streets.

My method of vision was entirely impartial: I was working directly with the evidences of vision, and not allowing suggestions outside the vision to predetermine my conclusions; I was entirely prepared to surprise myself. Even if the evidence ended up contradicting everything that had alighted upon me in my most tranquil delirium.

I know—from my own and singular witness—that in the beginning of this my work of searching I didn't have the slightest idea of the kind of language that would be slowly revealed to me until one day I could arrive at Constantinople. But I was already prepared to have to bear in the room the hot and humid season of our climate, and with it snakes, scorpions, tarantulas and myriads of mosquitoes that arise when a city collapses. And I knew that many times, in my work in the open field, I would have to share my bed with the livestock.

For now the sun was scorching me at the window. Only today had the sun fully reached me. But it was also true that only when the sun was reaching me could I, because I was standing, become a source of shade—where I would keep fresh wineskins of my water.

I would need a drill twelve meters long, camels, goats, and

sheep, an electric strip; and I would have to use the expanse itself directly because it would be impossible to reproduce, for example, in a simple aquarium, the richness of oxygen found on the surface of the oceans.

To keep my enthusiasm for the work from fading, I'd try not to forget that geologists already know that in the subsoil of the Sahara is an immense lake of potable water, I remember reading that; and that in the Sahara itself archeologists already unearthed the remains of household utensils and old settlements: seven thousand years ago, I had read, in that "region of fear" a prosperous agriculture had developed. The desert has a moistness that must be found again.

How should I set to work? to keep the dunes in place, I would have to plant two million green trees, especially eucalyptus—before bed I'd always read something, and I'd read a lot about the properties of the eucalyptus.

And I couldn't forget, at the outset of the job, to prepare myself to err. Not forgetting that the error had often become my path. Every time something I was thinking or feeling didn't work out—was because finally there was a breach, and, if I'd had courage before, I'd have already gone through it. But I'd always been afraid of delirium and error. My error, however, must be the path of a truth: since only when I err do I step out of what I know and what I understand. If "truth" were whatever I could understand—it would end up being just a small truth, one my size.

The truth must be exactly in what I shall never be able to understand. And, later, could I understand myself afterward? I don't know. Will the man of the future understand us as we are today? He distractedly, with some distracted tenderness, will pet our head as we do with the dog that comes over to us and looks at us from within its darkness, with mute and afflicted eyes. He, the future man, would pet us, remotely understanding us, as I remotely would understand myself later, beneath the memory of the memory of the memory already lost of a time of pain, not knowing that our time of pain would pass just as a child is not a static child, it's a growing being.

Anyway, beyond keeping the dunes in place with eucalyptus, I couldn't forget, if it turned out to be necessary, that rice prospers in brackish soil, whose high salt content it helps to cut down; I also was remembering that from my nightly readings that I, deliberately, tried to make impersonal so they would help me fall asleep.

And what other instruments would I need to dig? pickaxes, a hundred and fifty shovels, winches, even though I didn't exactly know what a winch was, heavy wagons with steel axles, a portable forge, besides nails and twine. As for my hunger, for my hunger I'd rely on the dates of ten million palms, not to mention almond and olive trees. And I'd have to know, beforehand, that, when praying from my minaret, I could only pray to the sands.

But I had probably been ready for the sands since birth: I'd know how to pray them, for that I wouldn't need to train beforehand, like witch-doctors who don't pray to things but pray things. I had always been prepared, trained as I had been by fear.

I remembered something engraved in my memory, and until that moment uselessly: that Arabs and nomads call the Sahara El Khela, the nothing, Tanesruft, the country of fear, Tiniri, land beyond the regions of pasture.

To pray the sands, I like them was already prepared by fear.

Once again too scorched, I sought the great blue lakes where

I plunged my withered eyes. Lakes or luminous stains of sky. The lakes were neither ugly nor beautiful. And that was just what was still terrifying my human. I tried to think about the Black Sea, I tried to think about the Persians descending the ravines—but in all of that I found neither beauty nor ugliness, just the infinite successions of centuries of the world.

Which, all of a sudden, I could no longer stand.

And I suddenly turned to the interior of the room which, in its burning, at least was not populated.

I SUDDENLY TURNED TO THE INTERIOR OF THE ROOM which, in its burning, at least was not populated.

No, during all that I hadn't been crazy or beside myself. It was just a visual meditation. The danger of meditating is accidentally beginning to think, and thinking is no longer meditating, thinking leads to an objective. The least dangerous thing, in meditation, is "seeing," which dispenses with thinking words. I know that an electronic microscope now exists that shows the image of an object one hundred and sixty thousand times larger than its natural size—but I wouldn't call the vision one has through that microscope hallucinatory, even if one no longer recognizes the small object that it monstrously enlarged.

If I was wrong in my visual meditation?

Absolutely probable. But also in my purely optical visions, of a chair or of a jug, I'm the victim of error: my visual witness of a jug or of a chair is defective in various ways. Error is one of my inevitable ways of working.

I sat back down on the bed. But now, looking at the roach,

I already knew much more.

Looking at it, I was seeing the vastness of the desert of Libya, in the region of Elschele. The roach that had reached that spot millennia before me, and also reached it before the dinosaurs. Faced with the roach, I could already see in the distance Damascus, the oldest city on the earth. In the desert of Libya, roaches and crocodiles? All that time I hadn't wanted to think what I had really already thought: that the roach is edible as a lobster, the roach is a crustacean.

And all I have is disgust for the crawling of crocodiles because I am not a crocodile. I am horrified by the crocodile's silence full of stratified scales.

But disgust is as necessary for me as the defilement of the waters is necessary for the reproduction of the things in the waters. Disgust guides me and fertilizes me. Through disgust, I see a night in Galilee. A night in Galilee is as if in the dark the breadth of the desert moved. The roach is a dark breadth moving.

I was already living the hell through which I was yet to pass, but I didn't know if all I had to do was pass through it, or if I'd have to stay there. I was already coming to know that this hell is horrible and good, maybe I myself wanted to stay there. Since I was seeing the deep and ancient life of the roach. I was seeing a silence that has the depth of an embrace. The sun is as much in the desert of Libya, as it is hot in itself. And the earth is the sun, how had I never seen that the earth is the sun?

And then it will happen—on a naked and dry rock in the desert of Libya—, the love of two roaches will happen. I now know what it's like. A roach waits. I see its brown-thing silence. And now—now I am seeing another roach moving slowly and with difficulty across the sands toward the rock.

Upon the rock, whose flood dried up millennia ago, two dry roaches. One is the silence of the other. The killers who meet: the world is extremely reciprocal. The quivering of an entirely mute rattling in the rock; and we, who made it to today, are still quivering with it.

—I promise this same silence for myself one day, I promise us what I now learned. Except for us it will have to be at night, for we are moist and salty beings, we are beings of seawater and tears. It will also be with the wholly open eyes of the roaches, but only if it is night, for I am a creature of great moist depths, I do not know the dust of dry cisterns, and the surface of a rock is not my home.

We are creatures that must plunge into the depth in order to breathe there, as the fish plunges in the water in order to breathe, except my depths are in the air of the night. Night is our latent state. And it is so moist that plants are born. In houses the lights go out in order to hear the crickets more clearly, and so the grasshoppers can walk atop the leaves almost without touching them, the leaves, the leaves, the leaves—in the night the soft anxiety is transmitted through the hollow of the air, the void is a means of transport.

Yes, not for us the love in the diurnal desert: we are the ones that swim, the night air is soggy and sweetened, and we are salty since sweating is our exhalation. Long ago I was drawn with you in a cave, and with you I swam from its dark depths up to today, I swam with my countless cilia—I was the oil that did not gush until today, when a black African woman drew me in my house, making me sprout upon a wall. Sleepwalking like the oil that gushes at last.

—I swear that's how love is. I know, only because I was sitting there and knowing. Only by the light of the roach, do I know that everything the two of us once had was already love. The roach had to hurt me as much as if my nails were being torn out—and then I could no longer stand the torture and confessed, and I'm informing. I could no longer stand it and am confessing that I already knew a truth that never had use or application, and that I would be afraid to apply, since I'm not grown-up enough to know how to use a truth without destroying myself.

If you could know through me, without having to be tortured first, without having to be split by the door of a wardrobe, without having broken your casings of fear that were drying with time into casings of stone, as mine had to be broken under the force of tongs until I reached the tender neutral of myself—if you could know through me … then learn from me, who had to be wholly exposed and lose all of my suitcases with their engraved initials.

—Guess at me, guess at me because it's cold, losing the lobster's casings is cold. Warm me up with your guesses about me, understand me because I am not understanding me. I am only loving the roach. And it's a hellish love.

But you're afraid, I know you were always afraid of the ritual. But when one has been tortured to the point of becoming a nucleus, then one starts demonically wanting to serve the ritual, even if the ritual means consuming oneself—just as in order to have the incense the only way to get it is to burn the incense. Listen, because I'm as serious as a roach that has cilia. Listen:

When one is one's own nucleus, one has no more deviations. Then one is one's own solemnity, and no longer fears consuming oneself when serving the consuming ritual—the ritual is the unfolding of the life of the nucleus, the ritual is not outside it: the ritual is inherent. The roach has its ritual within its cell. The ritual—believe me because I think I know—the ritual is the mark of the God. And every child is already born with the same ritual.

—I know: the two of us were always afraid of my solemnity and of your solemnity. We thought that it was a solemnity of form. And we always disguised what we knew: that living is always a question of life and death, hence the solemnity. We also knew, but without the gift of the grace of knowing it, that we are the life within us, and that we obey ourselves. The only destiny we are born with is that of the ritual. I had been calling the "mask" a lie, and it wasn't: it was the essential mask of solemnity. We would have to put on ritual masks to love one other. Scarabs are born with the mask with which they will fulfill themselves. Through original sin, we lost our mask.

I looked: the roach was a scarab. It was entirely only its own mask. Through the profound absence of the roach's laughter, I was seeing its warrior ferocity. It was meek but its function was fierce.

I am meek but my function in living is fierce. Ah, pre-human love invades me. I understand, I understand! The form of living is a secret so secret that it is the silent crawling of a secret. It's a secret in the desert. And I certainly already knew. Since, by the light of the love of two roaches there came to me the memory of a true love I once had and that I didn't know I'd had—since love then was something I understood with a word. But there is something that must be said, it must be said.

BUT THERE IS SOMETHING THAT MUST BE SAID, IT must be said.

—I'm going to say what I never said to you before, maybe that's what's missing: having said. If I didn't say it, it wasn't out of greed in telling, or because of my muteness of a roach that has more eyes than mouth. If I didn't say it it's because I didn't know that I knew—but I know now. I'm going to say to you that I love you. I know that I said that to you before, and that it was also true when I said it, but only now am I really saying it. I have to say it before I ... Oh, but it's the roach that's going to die, not I! I don't need this letter from a cell on death row....

—No, I don't want to give you the fright of my love. If you're afraid of me, I'll be afraid of me. Don't be scared of the pain. I'm now as certain as the certainty that in that room I was alive and the roach was alive: I'm certain of this: that all things course above and below pain. Pain is not the true name for whatever people call pain. Listen: I'm certain of it.

Since, now that I was no longer struggling with myself, I quietly knew that that was a roach, that pain was not pain.

Ah, if only I'd known what was going to happen in the room, and had picked up more cigarettes before coming in: I was consuming myself with the will to smoke.

—Ah, if I could transmit the memory to you, the memory that's just now come alive, of what the two of us had lived without being aware of it. Do you want to remember with me? oh, I know it's hard: but let's go toward ourselves. Instead of surpassing ourselves. Don't be afraid now, you're safe because at least it already happened, unless you see danger in knowing that it happened.

It's that, when we loved, I didn't know that love was happening much more exactly when the thing we were calling love wasn't there. The neutral of love, that was what we were living and despising.

What I'm talking about is when nothing was happening, and, we called that nothing-happening an interval. But what was that interval like?

It was the enormous flower opening, all swollen with itself, my great and trembling vision. What I was watching, was immediately clotting beneath my gaze and becoming mine—but not a permanent clot: if I pressed it between my hands, like a bit of clotted blood, the solidification would liquefy again into blood between my fingers.

And time wasn't totally liquid because, for me to gather things with my hands, things had to coagulate like fruits. In the intervals we called empty and calm, and when we thought that the love had stopped …

I remember the soreness in my throat back then: tonsils swollen, clotting within me was swift. And could easily liquefy: my sore throat went away, I was telling you. Like glaciers in summertime, and liquefied the rivers run. Every word of ours—in the time we called empty—each word was as light and empty as a butterfly: the word from inside fluttering out to meet the mouth, the words were said but we didn't even hear them because the melting glaciers made so much noise as they ran. Amidst the liquid din, our mouths were moving speaking, and in fact we only saw the moving mouths but didn't hear them—we each looked at the mouth of the other, seeing it speak, and it hardly mattered that we didn't hear, oh, in the name of God it hardly mattered.

And in our name, it was enough to see the mouth speaking, and we laughed because we were hardly paying attention. And yet we were calling that not-listening indifference and lack of love.

But we actually were speaking and how! speaking the nothing. Yet everything shimmered as when heavy tears stick in the eyes; that is why everything shimmered.

In those intervals we were thinking of ourselves as resting from one being the other. Really it was the great pleasure of not being the other: since that way each of us had two. Everything was going to end, when what we called the interval of love ended; and because it was going to end, it weighed tremulous beneath the very weight of its ending already in itself. I remember all this as through a quake of water.

Ah, could it be that we were not originally human? and that, out of practical necessity, we became human? that horrifies me, as it does you. Since the roach was looking at me with its scarab carapace, with its broken body made completely of pipes and of antennae and flabby cement—and that was undeniably a truth prior to our words, that was undeniably the life that up till then I had not wanted.

—Then—then through the door of damnation, I ate life

and was eaten by life. I was understanding that my kingdom is of this world. And I understood that through the hell inside me. Because inside myself I saw what hell is like.

BECAUSE INSIDE MYSELF I SAW WHAT HELL IS LIKE.
Hell is the mouth that bites and eats the living flesh with its blood, and the one being eaten howls with delight in his eye: hell is pain as delight of the matter, and with the laughter of delight, the tears run in pain. And the tear that comes from the laughter of pain is the opposite of redemption. I was seeing the inexorability of the roach with its ritual mask. I was seeing that that was hell: the cruel acceptance of pain, the solemn lack of pity for one's own destiny, loving the ritual of life more than one's own self—that was hell, where the one eating the other's living face was indulging in the joy of pain.

For the first time I was feeling with hellish voracity the desire to have had the children I never had: I wanted to have reproduced, not in three or four children, but in twenty thousand my organic hellishness full of pleasure. My future survival in children would be my true present, which is, not just myself, but my pleasurable species never interrupted. Not having had children left me spasmodic as if confronting an addiction denied.

That roach had had children and I had not: the roach could

125

die crushed, but I was condemned never to die, since if I died, even just once, I would die. And I wanted not to die but to remain eternally dying as the delight of supreme pain. I was in hell pierced with pleasure like a low buzz of nerves of pleasure.

And all that—oh, my horror—all that was happening in the wide heart of indifference.... All that losing oneself in a spiraling destiny, and that does not get lost. In that infinite destiny, made only of cruel present, I, like a larva—in my deepest inhumanity, since until then what had escaped me was my real inhumanity—I and we like larvae devour ourselves in soft flesh.

And there is no punishment! That is hell: there is no punishment. Since in hell we make the supreme delight of what would be punishment, in this desert we make of punishment yet another ecstasy of laughter with tears, in hell we make of punishment a hope for delight.

So was this the other side of humanization and hope?

In hell, that demonic faith for which I am not responsible. And which is faith in orgiastic life. The orgy of hell is the apotheosis of the neutral. The joy of the Sabbath is the joy of getting lost in the atonal.

What still frightened me was that even the unpunishable horror would be generously reabsorbed by the abyss of unending time, by the abyss of unending heights, by the deep abyss of the God: absorbed into the heart of an indifference.

So unlike human indifference. Since that was a self-serving-indifference, a fulfilled indifference. It was an extremely energetic indifference. And all in silence, in that hell of mine. Since laughter forms part of the volume of the silence, only in the eye sparkled the indifferent-pleasure, but laughter was in the blood itself and cannot be heard.

And all this is in this very instant, it is in the now. Yet at the same time the present instant is entirely remote because of the size-grandeur of the God. Because of the enormous perpetual size, even whatever exists right now, is remote: in the very instant that the roach is broken in the wardrobe, it too is remote in relation to the heart of the great self-seeking-indifference that reabsorbs it with impunity.

The grandiose indifference—was that what was existing inside me?

The hellish grandeur of life: since not even my body delimits me, mercy does not let my body delimit me. In hell, my body does not delimit me, and is that what I call soul? Living the life that is no longer the life of my body—is that what I call impersonal soul?

And my impersonal soul burns me. The grandiose indifference of a star is the soul of the roach, the star is the very exorbitance of the body of the roach. The roach and I aspire to a peace that cannot be ours—it's a peace beyond the size and destiny of the roach and of me. And because my soul is so unlimited that it is no longer me, and because it is so beyond me—because I am always remote to myself, I am as unreachable to myself as a star is unreachable to me. I contort myself to try to reach the present time that surrounds me, but I am still remote in relation to this very instant. The future, alas, is closer to me than the instant now.

The roach and I are hellishly free because our living matter is greater than we are, we are hellishly free because my own life is so barely containable inside my body that I cannot use it. My life is used more by the earth than by me, I am so much greater than whatever I used to call "I" that, just by having the life of the world, I would have myself. It would take a horde of roaches to make a slightly sensitive spot in the world—yet one single roach, just through its attention-life, that single roach is the world.

The whole most unreachable part of my soul and which does not belong to me—is the one that touches my border with whatever is no longer I, and to which I give myself. All my anguish has been this unsurpassable and excessively close closeness. I am more whatever within me is not.

And that's when the hand I was holding abandoned me. No, no. I am the one who pulled my hand away because now I must go alone.

If I manage to return from the kingdom of life I shall take your hand again, and kiss it gratefully because it waited for me, and waited for my path to go by, and for me to return thin, ravenous and humble: hungry only for the little, hungry only for the less.

Because, sitting and unmoving there, I had started wanting to live my own remoteness as the only way of living my present. And that, which is apparently innocent, that was once again a pleasure that resembled a horrendous and cosmic delight.

To relive it, I let go of your hand.

Because in that enjoyment there was no pity. Pity is being the child of someone or of some thing—but being the world is the cruelty. Cockroaches gnaw each other and kill each other and penetrate each other in procreation and eat each other in an eternal summer that darkens into night—hell is a summer that boils and almost darkens into night. The present does not see the roach, the present time looks at it from such a great distance that it does not perceive the roach from the heights, and only sees a silent desert—the present time does not even suspect, in the naked desert, the orgiastic festival of gypsies.

Where, reduced to small jackals, we eat each other with

laughter. With the laughter of pain—and free. The mystery of human destiny is that we are inevitable, but we have the freedom to carry out or not our inevitability: it depends on us to carry out our inevitable destiny. While inhuman beings, like the roach, carry out their own complete cycle, without ever erring because they do not choose. But it depends on me to freely become whatever I inevitably am. I am the mistress of my inevitability, and, if I decide not to carry it out, I shall remain outside my specifically living nature. But if I carry out my neutral and living nucleus, then, within my species, I shall be being specifically human.

—But becoming human can be transformed into an ideal, and suffocate beneath accretions.... To be human ought not be an ideal for man who is inevitably human, being human must be the way that I, living thing, obeying freely the path of whatever is alive, am human. And I don't even need to care for my soul, it will inevitably care for me, and I don't have to make a soul for myself: all I have to do is choose to live. We are free, and that is hell. But there are so many roaches that they appear a prayer.

My kingdom is of this world ... and my kingdom was not only human. I knew. But knowing that would scatter death-life, and a child in my womb would be vulnerable to being eaten by life-death itself, and without a Christian word making sense.... But there are so many children in the womb that they appear a prayer.

At that moment I had still not understood that the first sketch of what would become a prayer was already being born from the happy hell I had entered, and which I no longer wanted to depart.

From that country of rats and tarantulas and roaches, my

love, where enjoyment drips in fat drops of blood.

Only the mercy of the God could yank me out of that terrible indifferent joy in which I was bathing, complete.

For I was exulting. I was coming to know the violence of the happy dark—I was happy as a demon, hell is my maximum.

HELL IS MY MAXIMUM.

I was fully in the heart of an indifference that is still and alert. And in the heart of an indifferent love, of an indifferent waking sleep, of an indifferent pain. Of a God who, if I loved Him, I didn't understand what He wanted from me. I know, He wanted me to be his equal, and for me to equal Him through a love of which I was incapable.

Through a love so great that it would be of such an indifferent personal—as if I were not a person. He wanted for me to be the world with Him. He wanted my human divinity, and that had to start with an initial stripping-down of the constructed human.

And I had taken the first step: since at least I already knew that being a human is a sensitization, an orgasm of nature. And that, only through an anomaly of nature, instead of being the God, as other beings are He, instead of being He, we wanted to see Him. It would not hurt to see Him, if we were as great as He. A roach is greater than I because its life is so given over to Him that it comes from the infinite and goes toward the infinite without noticing, it doesn't miss a beat.

I had taken the first great step. But what had happened to me?

I had fallen into the temptation of seeing, the temptation of knowing and feeling. My grandeur, searching for the grandeur of the God, had taken me to the grandeur of hell. I had not been able to understand His organization except through the spasm of a demonic exultation. Curiosity had expelled me from the shelter—and I was finding the indifferent God who is all good because He is neither bad nor good, I was in the heart of matter that is the indifferent explosion of itself. Life was having the strength of a titanic indifference. A titanic indifference that wanted to advance. And I, who wanted to advance with it, had been hooked on the pleasure that was making me merely hellish.

The temptation of pleasure. The temptation is to eat directly from the source. The temptation is to eat directly from the law. And the punishment is no longer wanting to stop eating, and eating oneself who am equally edible matter. And I was seeking damnation like a happiness. I was seeking the most orgiastic in myself. I would never rest again: I had stolen the hunting horse of a king of joy. I was now worse than myself!

I shall never rest again: I stole the hunting horse from the Sabbath king. If I fall asleep for an instant, the echo of a whinny wakes me. And it is useless not to go. In the dark of night the panting gives me goose bumps. I pretend to sleep but in the silence the steed breathes. It says nothing but it breathes, waits and breathes. Every day it will be the same thing: right at dusk I start to get melancholy and thoughtful. I know that the first drum on the mountain will make the night, I know that the third will already wrap me in its thunder.

And by the fifth drum I shall already be unconscious inside my greed. Until at dawn, by the last lightest drums, I shall end up without knowing how beside a creek, without ever knowing what I did, beside the enormous and tired head of the horse.

Tired from what? What did we do, we who trot in the hell of joy? I have not gone for two centuries. The last time I got down from the adorned saddle, my human sadness was so great that I swore never again. Yet the trotting carries on inside me. I chat, tidy the house, smile, but I know that the trot is inside me. I miss it like one who dies. I can no longer not go.

And I know at night, when it calls me, I shall go. I want just one more time for the horse to lead my thought. That was who I learned with. If you can call it thought, that hour between barks. The dogs bark, I start to get sad because I know, with my eye already shining, that I shall go. When at night it calls me to hell, I go. I come down like a cat on the roofs. Nobody knows, nobody sees. I turn up in the dark, mute and aglow. Fifty-three flutes run after us. Ahead of us a clarinet lights us. And nothing more is given to me to know.

At dawn I shall see us exhausted beside the creek, without knowing what crimes we committed before reaching the dawn. In my mouth and on your hooves the mark of blood. What did we sacrifice? At dawn I shall be standing beside the mute steed, with the first bells of a Church flowing down the creek, with the remains of the flutes still flowing from my hair.

The night is my life, darkness falls, the happy night is my sad life—steal, steal the steed from me because after stealing so much I have even stolen the dawn, and made a premonition from it: swiftly steal the steed while there's still time, before darkness falls, if there still is time, because when I stole the steed I had to kill the King, and in murdering him I stole the death of the King. And the joy of the murder consumes me with pleasure.

I was eating myself, I who am also living matter of the Sabbath.

I WAS EATING MYSELF, I WHO AM ALSO LIVING MATTER of the Sabbath.

Could that have been, though much more than that, the temptation of the saints? And from which he who would or would not be a saint, emerges sanctified or does not. From that temptation in the desert, I, laywoman, the unsaint, would succumb or emerge from it for the first time as a living being.

—Listen, there's something called human sainthood, and which is not that of the saints. I'm afraid that not even the God understands that human sainthood is more dangerous than divine sainthood, that the sainthood of the laity is more painful. Yet Christ himself knew that if they had done what they did to Him, they would do much more to us, since He said: "For if they do these things in a green tree, what shall be done in the dry?"

Trial. Now I understand what a trial is. Trial: it means that life is trying me. But trial: means that I too am trying. And trying can become an ever more insatiable thirst.

Wait for me: I'm going to pull you out of the hell into which I descended. Listen, listen:

Since from the delight without reprieve, a sob was already being born inside me that seemed more like a sob of joy. It wasn't a sob of pain, I had never heard it before: it was that of my life splitting in order to procreate me. In those desert sands I was starting to be of the daintiness of a first shy offering, like that of a flower. What was I offering? what could I offer of myself—I, who was being the desert, I, who had asked and had?

I was offering the sob. I was finally crying inside my hell. I use and sweat the very wings of blackness, and was using them and sweating them for me—which art Thou, thou, flash of silence. I am not Thou, but me art Thou. Only for that I shall never be able to feel Thee directly: because Thou art me.

Oh, God, I was starting to understand with enormous surprise: that my hellish orgy was human torment itself.

How could I have guessed? if I didn't know that one laughs in suffering. Because I didn't know that that was how one suffered. So I had called joy my deepest suffering.

And in the sob the God came to me, the God was occupying all of me now. I was offering my hell to God. The first sob had made—of my terrible pleasure and of my feast—a new pain: that now was as light and helpless as the flower of my own desert. The tears that were flowing now were like those for a love. The God, who could never be understood by me except as I understood Him: breaking me like a flower that at birth can barely hold itself up and seems to break.

But now, that I knew that my joy had been suffering, I was wondering if I was fleeing toward a God because I couldn't stand my humanity. Because I needed someone who wasn't petty like me, someone who was so much wider than I in order to allow my misfortune without even using pity and solace—someone who was, who was! and not, like me, an accuser of nature, not like me, a person astonished by the power of my own hates and loves.

Right this second, now, a doubt surprises me. God, or whatever Thou art called: I only ask for help now: but for Thou to help me now not darkly as Thou art me, but clearly this time and in plain sight.

Since I need to know exactly this: am I feeling what I am feeling, or am I feeling what I would like to feel? or am I feeling what I might need to feel?

Because I no longer even want the concretization of an ideal, what I want to be is just a seed. Even if afterwards from that seed ideals are born again, either the real ones, which are the birth of a path, or the false ones, which are the accretions. Could I be feeling what I would like to feel? Since a millimeter's difference is enormous, and that millimeter of space can save me through truth or once again make me lose everything I saw. It's dangerous. Men praise highly what they feel. Which is as dangerous as detesting what one feels.

I had offered my hell to the God. And my cruelty, my love, my cruelty had suddenly stopped. And suddenly that same desert was the still-vague sketch of what was called paradise. The moisture of a paradise. Not another thing, but that same desert. And I was surprised as one is surprised by a light that comes out of the nothing.

Was I understanding that what I had experienced, that nucleus of hellish rapacity, was that what is called love? But—neutral-love?

Neutral love. The neutral was whispering. I was reaching what I had sought all my life: whatever is the most final identity and that I had called inexpressive. That was what had always been in my eyes in the snapshot: an inexpressive joy, a pleasure that does not know that it is pleasure—a pleasure too delicate for my coarse humanity that had always been made of coarse concepts.

—I made such an effort to speak to myself of a hell that has no words. Now, how shall I speak of a love that only has whatever one feels, and before which the word "love" is a dusty object?

The hell I had gone through—how can I explain it to you?—had been the hell that comes from love. Ah, people put the idea of sin in sex. But how innocent and childish that sin is. The real hell is that of love. Love is the experience of a danger of greater sin—it is the experience of the mud and the degradation and the worst joy. Sex is the fright of a child. But how shall I speak for myself about the love that I now knew?

It's almost impossible. Because in the neutral of love is a continual joy, like a noise of leaves in the wind. And I fit into the neutral nakedness of the woman on the wall. The same neutral, the one that had consumed me in pernicious and eager joy, it was in that same neutral that I now was hearing another kind of continual joy of love. Whatever God is was more in the neutral noise of the leaves in the wind than in my old human prayer.

Unless I could make the real prayer, and which to others and myself would resemble the kabbalah of a black magic, a neutral murmur.

That murmur, without any human meaning, would be my identity touching the identity of things. I know that, in relation to the human, that neutral prayer would be a monstrosity. But in relation to whatever is God, it would be: being.

I had been forced into the desert to find out with horror that the desert is alive, to find out that a roach is life. I had drawn back until I found out that in me the deepest life is before the human—and for that I had had the diabolic courage to get rid of feelings. I had to give no human value to life in order to understand the breadth, much more than the human breadth, of the God. Had I asked for the most dangerous and forbidden thing? risking my soul, would I have boldly demanded to see God?

And now it was as if I were before Him and didn't understand—I was standing uselessly before Him, and I was once again before the nothing. To me, as to everyone, everything had been given, but I wanted more: I wanted to know about that everything. And I had sold my soul in order to find out. But now I was understanding that I had not sold it to the devil, but much more dangerously: to God. Who had let me see. Since He knew that I would not know how to see whatever I saw: the explanation of an enigma is the repetition of the enigma. What art Thou? and the answer is: Thou art. What do Thou existest? and the answer is: what thou existest. I had the ability to ask the question, but not to hear the answer.

No, I had not even known how to ask the question. Yet the answer had imposed itself upon me since I was born. Because of this continual answer I, the wrong way around, had been forced to seek the corresponding question. So I had got lost in a labyrinth of questions, and asked questions at random, hoping that one of them would occasionally correspond to the answer, and that I could then understand the answer.

But I was like a person who, having been born blind and not having anyone around who could see, that person could not even form a question about vision: she wouldn't know that seeing existed. But, since vision actually did exist, even if that person didn't know about it and had never even heard of it, that person would be motionless, restless, alert, not knowing how to ask about something she didn't know existed—she would feel the lack of something that should have been hers.

SHE WOULD FEEL THE LACK OF SOMETHING THAT
should have been hers.

—No. I didn't tell you everything. I still wanted to see if I
could get away with only telling myself a little. But my libera-
tion will only come about if I have the immodesty of my own
incomprehension.

Because, sitting on the bed, I then said to myself:

—They gave me everything, and just look what everything
is! it's a roach that is alive and that is about to die. And then
I looked at the door handle. After that I looked at the wood
of the wardrobe. I looked at the glass of the window. Just look
at what everything is: it's a piece of thing, a piece of iron, of
gravel, of glass. I said to myself: look what I fought for, to have
exactly what I already had, I crawled until the doors opened
for me, the doors of the treasure I was seeking: and look what
the treasure was!

The treasure was a piece of metal, it was a piece of whitewash from the wall, it was a piece of matter made into roach.

Since prehistory I had started my march through the desert,

and without a star to guide me, only perdition guiding me, only going astray guiding me—until, almost dead from the ecstasy of fatigue, illuminated by passion, I finally found the safe. And in the safe, sparkling with glory, the hidden secret. The most remote secret in the world, opaque, but blinding me with the irradiation of its simple existence, sparkling there with glory that hurt my eyes. Inside the safe the secret:

A piece of thing.

A piece of iron, a roach's antenna, a plaster chip.

My exhaustion was prostrate at the feet of the piece of thing, hellishly adoring. The secret of power was power, the secret of love was love—and the jewel of the world is an opaque piece of thing.

The opacity was reverberating in my eyes. The secret of my millennial trajectory of orgy and death and glory and thirst until I finally found what I had always had, and for that I had had to die first. Ah, I am being so direct that I manage to seem symbolic.

A piece of thing? the secret of the pharaohs. And for that secret I had almost given my life …

More, much more: to have that secret, that even now I still did not understand, I would give my life again. I had risked the world in search of the question that follows the answer. An answer that was still a secret, even once the corresponding question was revealed. I had not found a human answer to the enigma. But much more, oh, much more: I had found the enigma itself. I had been given too much. What would I do with what had been given to me? "May the holy thing not be given to the dogs."

And I was not even touching the thing. I was just touching the space that goes from me to the vital node—I was within the zone of cohesive and controlled vibration of the vital node.

The vital node vibrates at the vibration of my arrival.

My greatest possible approach stops a step away. What prevents that step from being taken? It is the opaque irradiation, simultaneously from the thing and from me. Because we are similar, we repel one other; because we are similar we cannot enter the other. And if the step were taken?

I don't know, I don't know. Since the thing can never really be touched. The vital node is a finger pointing at it—and, the thing being pointed at, wakens like a milligram of radium in the tranquil dark. Then the wet crickets are heard. The light of the milligram does not alter the dark. Because the dark is not illuminable, the dark is a way of being: the dark is in the vital node of the dark, and you cannot touch the vital node of a thing.

Would the thing for me have to reduce itself to being just whatever surrounds the untouchable part of the thing? My God, give me what Thou hast done. Or hast Thou already given it to me? and I am the one who cannot take the step that will give me what Thou hast done? Am I what Thou hast made? and I cannot take the step toward me, me that art Thing and Thou. Give me what Thou art in me. Give me what Thou art in others, Thou art the he, I know, I know because when I touch I see the he. But the he, the man, takes care of what Thou hast given him and covers himself in a casing made especially for me to touch and see. And I want more than the casing that I love too. I want what I Thee love.

But I had only found, beyond the casing, the enigma itself. And was trembling all over for fear of the God.

I tremble in fear and adoration of whatever exists.

Whatever exists, and which is just a piece of thing, yet I must place my hand over my eyes against the opacity of that thing. Ah, the violent loving unconsciousness of whatever exists surpasses the possibility of my consciousness. I am afraid of so much matter—the matter vibrates with attention, vibrates with process, vibrates with inherent present time. Whatever exists beats in strong waves against the unbreakable grain that I am, and that grain whirls between abysses of calm billows of existence, it whirls and does not dissolve, that grain-seed.

What am I the seed of? Seed of thing, seed of existence, seed of those very billows of neutral-love. I, person, am an embryo. The embryo is only sensitive—that is its only particular inherence. The embryo hurts. The embryo is eager and shrewd. My eagerness is my most initial hunger: I am pure because I am eager.

Of the embryo that I am, this joyful matter is also made: the thing. Which is an existence satisfied with its own process, deeply occupied with no more than its own process, and the process vibrates entirely. That piece of thing inside the safe is the secret of the coffer. And the coffer itself is also made of the same secret, the safe holding the jewel of the world, the safe too is made of the same secret.

Ah, and I don't want any of this! I hate what I managed to see. I don't want that world made of thing!

I don't want it. But I cannot help feeling all enlarged inside myself by the poverty of the opaque and the neutral: the thing is alive like weeds. And if that is hell, it is heaven itself: the choice is mine. I am the one who shall be demonic or angel; if I am demonic, this is hell; if I am angel, this is heaven. Ah, I send my angel to prepare the path before me. No, not my angel: but my humanity and its compassion.

I sent my angel to prepare the path before me and to let the stones know of my coming and for them to soften before my incomprehension.

And my gentlest angel was who found the piece of thing. It couldn't find anything except what it was. Since even when something falls from the sky, it is a meteorite, that is, a piece of thing. My angel lets me be the worshipper of a piece of iron or glass.

But I am the one who must stop myself from giving a name to the thing. The name is an accretion, and blocks contact with the thing. The name of the thing is an interval for the thing. The desire for the accretion is great—because the naked thing is so tedious.

BECAUSE THE NAKED THING IS SO TEDIOUS.

Ah, so that was why I had always had a kind of love for tedium. And a continual hatred of it.

Because tedium is saltless and resembles the thing itself. And I had not been great enough: only the great love monotony. Contact with supersound of the atonal has an inexpressive joy that only flesh, in love, tolerates. The great have the vital quality of flesh, and, not only tolerate the atonal, they aspire to it.

My old constructions had consisted in continually trying to transform the atonal into tonal, in dividing the infinite into a series of finites, and without noticing that finite is not a quantity, it is a quality. And my great discomfort in all that had been feeling that, no matter how long the series of finites, it did not exhaust the residual quality of the infinite.

But tedium—tedium had been the only way I could feel the atonal. And I just had not known that I liked tedium because I suffered from it. But in living matter, suffering is not the measure of life: suffering is the fatal by-product and, no matter how sharp, is negligible.

Oh, and I who should have noticed all that long before! I, who had as my secret theme the inexpressive. An inexpressive face fascinated me; the moment that was not the climax attracted me. Nature, what I liked about nature, was its vibrating inexpressiveness.

—Ah, I don't know how to tell you, since I only get eloquent when I err, error leads me to argue and think. But how to speak to you, if there is a silence when I get it right? How to speak to you of the inexpressive?

Even in tragedy, since the true tragedy is in the inexorability of its inexpressiveness, which is its naked identity.

Sometimes—sometimes we ourselves manifest the inexpressive—one does that in art, in bodily love as well—to manifest the inexpressive is to create. In the end we are so so happy! since there is not just one way of entering into contact with life, there are even negative ways! even painful ones, even almost impossible ones—and all that, all that before dying, all that even while we are awake! And there is also sometimes the exasperation of the atonal, which is of a deep joy: the exasperated atonal is the flight taking off—nature is the exasperated atonal, that was how the worlds formed: the atonal got exasperated.

And consider the leaves, how green and heavy they are, they got exasperated in thing, how blind the leaves are and how green they are. And feel in the hand how everything has a weight, the weight does not escape the inexpressive hand. Do not awaken the person who is entirely absent, who is absorbed is feeling the weight of things. Weight is one of the proofs of the thing: only things with weight can fly. And the only things that fall—the celestial meteorite—are those that have weight.

Or is all that still me wanting the delight of the words of things? or is that still me wanting the orgasm of extreme beauty, of understanding, of the extreme gesture of love?

Because tedium is of a too primary joy! And that is why heaven is intolerable to me. And I don't want heaven, I miss hell! I'm not up to staying in heaven because heaven has no human taste! it has the taste of thing, and the vital thing has no taste, like blood in my mouth when I cut myself and suck the blood, I am frightened because my own blood has no human taste.

And mother's milk, which is human, mother's milk is much before the human, and has no taste, it is nothing, I already tried it—it is like the sculpted eye of a statue that is empty and has no expression, since when art is good it is because it touched upon the inexpressive, the worst art is expressive, that art which trangresses the piece of iron and the piece of glass, and the smile, and the scream.

—Ah, hand holding mine, if I hadn't needed so much of myself to shape my life, I would already have had life!

But that, as far as humans are concerned, would be destruction: living life instead of living one's own life is forbidden. It is a sin to enter the divine matter. And that sin has an irremediable punishment: one who dares to enter this secret, in losing individual life, disorganizes the human world. I too could have left my solid constructions in the air, even knowing that they were dismantlable—if not for the temptation. And the temptation can keep one from crossing to the other shore.

But why not stay inside, without trying to cross to the opposite shore? Staying inside the thing is madness. I do not want to stay inside, or else my previous humanization, which was so gradual, would come to have had no basis.

And I do not want to lose my humanity! ah, losing it hurts, my love, like casting off a still-living body and that refuses to die like the severed pieces of a lizard.

But now it was too late. I would have to be greater than my fear, and I would have to see what my previous humanization was made of. Ah, I must believe with so much faith in the true and hidden seed of my humanity, that I must not fear seeing humanization from the inside.

I MUST NOT FEAR SEEING HUMANIZATION FROM THE inside.

—Give me your hand once again, I still don't know how to comfort myself about the truth.

But—sit with me for a moment—the greatest lack of belief in the truth of humanization would be to think that the truth would destroy humanization. Wait for me, wait: I know that later I'll know how to fit all this into daily practicality, don't forget that I too need a daily life!

But see, my love, the truth cannot be bad. The truth is what it is—and, exactly because it is immutably what it is, it must be our great security, just as having desired our father or mother is so inevitable that it must have been our foundation. So then, understand? why would I be afraid of eating the good and the evil? if they exist that is because that is what exists.

Wait for me, I know I'm heading for some thing that hurts because I am losing others—but wait for me to go a little further. From all that, perhaps, a name could be born! a name without word, but that might implant the truth in my human makeup.

Don't be afraid as I am afraid: it cannot be bad to have seen life in its plasma. It is dangerous, it is sinful, but it cannot be bad because we are made of that plasma.

—Listen, don't be afraid: remember that I ate of the forbidden fruit and yet was not struck down by the orgy of being. So, listen: that means I shall find even greater refuge than if I had not eaten of life.... Listen, because I dived into the abyss I started to love the abyss of which I am made. Identity can be dangerous because of the intense pleasure that could become mere pleasure. But now I'm accepting loving the thing!

And it's not dangerous, I swear it's not dangerous.

Since the state of grace exists permanently: we are always saved. All the world is in a state of grace. A person is only struck down by sweetness when realizing that we are in grace, the gift is feeling that we are in grace, and few risk recognizing that within themselves. But there is no danger of perdition, I know now: the state of grace is inherent.

—Listen. I was only used to transcending. Hope for me was postponement. I had never let my soul free, and had quickly organized myself as a person because it is too risky to lose the form. But I now see what was really happening to me: I had so little faith that I had invented merely the future, I believed so little in whatever exists that I was delaying the present for a promise and for a future.

But now I discover that one doesn't even need hope.

It's much more serious. Ah, I know I am once again meddling with danger and should shut up to myself. One shouldn't say that hope is not necessary, because that could transform itself, since I am weak, into a destructive weapon. And for yourself, into a useful weapon of destruction.

I could not understand and you could not understand that dispensing with hope—really means action, and today. No, it is not destructive, wait, let me understand us. It is a forbidden subject not because it is bad but because we risk ourselves.

I know that if I abandoned what was a life entirely organized around hope, I know that abandoning all that—in favor of that wider thing which is being alive—abandoning all that hurts like separating from a child not yet born. Hope is a child not yet born, only promised, and that bruises.

But I know that at the same time I want and no longer want to contain myself. It's like death throes: some thing in death wants to break free and yet fears letting go of the safety of the body. I know it is dangerous to speak of the lack of hope, but listen—a deep alchemy is happening in me, and it was in the fire of hell that it was forged. And that gives me the greatest right: to err.

Listen without fright and without suffering: the neutral of the God is so great and vital that I, unable to stand the cell of the God, I had humanized it. I know it is horribly dangerous to discover now that the God has the power of the impersonal—because I know, oh, I know! that it's as if that meant the destruction of the plea!

And it is as if the future stopped coming to exist. And we cannot, we are needy.

But listen for a moment: I am not speaking of the future, I am speaking of a permanent present. And that means that hope does not exist because it is no longer a postponed future, it is today. Because the God does not promise. He is much greater than that: He is, and never stops being. We are the ones who cannot stand this always present light, and so we promise it for later, just in order not to feel it today, right this very minute. The present is the face today of the God. The horror is that we know that we see God in life itself. It is with our eyes fully open that we see God. And if I postpone the face of reality until after my death—it's out of guile, because I prefer to be dead when it is time to see Him and that way I think I shall not really see Him, just as I only have the courage to really dream when I sleep.

I know that what I am feeling is serious and could destroy me. Because—because it is like giving myself the news that the kingdom of heaven already is.

And I don't want the kingdom of heaven, I don't want it, all I can stand is the promise of it! The news I am getting from myself sounds cataclysmic to me, and once again nearly demonic. But it is only out of fear. It is fear. Since relinquishing hope means that I shall have to start living, and not just promise myself life. And this is the greatest fright I can have. I used to hope. But the God is today: his kingdom already began.

And his kingdom, my love, is also of this world. I did not have the courage to stop being a promise, and I was promising myself, like an adult who lacks the courage to see she is already an adult and keeps promising herself maturity.

And so I was realizing that the divine promise of life is already being honored, and that it always was. Before, only once in a while, I was reminded, in an instantaneous and immediately shunned vision, that the promise is not only for the future, it is yesterday and it is permanently today: but that was shocking to me. I preferred to keep asking, without the courage to already have.

And I do. I always will. All I have to do is need, and I have. Needing never ends since needing is inherent to my neutral. Whatever I do with the plea and the want—that will be the life I will have made from my life. Not putting oneself in view of hope is not the destruction of the plea! and is not abstaining from neediness. Ah, it's by increasing it, it's by infinitely increasing the plea that is born of neediness.

INFINITELY INCREASING THE PLEA THAT IS BORN OF
neediness.

It is not for us that the cow's milk flows, but we drink it. The flower was not made for us to look at it or for us to smell its fragrance, and we look at it and smell it. The Milky Way does not exist for us to know of its existence, but we know of it. And we know God. And what we need from Him, we elicit. (I don't know what I am calling God, but thus he may be called.) If we only know very little of God, that is because we need little: we only have of Him whatever is inevitably enough for us, we only have of God whatever fits inside us. (Nostalgia is not for the God we are missing, it is the nostalgia for ourselves who are not enough; we miss our impossible grandeur—my unreachable present is my paradise lost.)

We suffer from being so little hungry, though our small hunger is enough for us to deeply miss the pleasure we would have if our hunger were greater. We only drink as much milk as the body needs, and of the flower we only see as far as our eyes and their flat fullness go. The more we need, the more

God exists. The more we can take, the more God we shall have.

He lets us. (He was not born for us, neither were we born for Him, we and He are at the same time). He is uninterruptedly busy with being, as all things are being but He does not keep us from joining Him, and, with Him, be busy being, in such a fluid and steady interchange—like that of living. He, for example, He uses us totally because there is nothing in each of us that He, whose necessity is absolutely infinite, does not need. He uses us, and does not prevent us from using Him. The ore that is in the earth is not responsible for not being used.

We are very behind, and have no idea how to take advantage of God in an interchange—as if we still had not discovered that milk can be drunk. A few centuries on or a few minutes on we might say astonished: and to think that God always was! the one who barely was was me—just as we would say of oil that we finally needed it enough to know how to wrest it from the earth, just as one day we shall regret those who died of cancer without using the cure that is there. Clearly we still do not need to not die of cancer. Everything is here. (Beings from another planet might already know things and live in an interchange that for them is natural; for us, meanwhile, the interchange would be "holiness" and would completely unsettle our life.)

The cow's milk, we drink it. And if the cow does not let us, we resort to violence. (In life and in death everything is lawful, living is always a matter of life and death.) With God we can also force our way through violence. He Himself, when He more especially needs one of us, He chooses us and violates us.

Except my violence toward God must be toward myself. I must violate myself in order to need more. In order to become so desperately greater that I end up empty and indigent. Thus shall I have touched the root of needing. The great emptiness in me shall be my place for existing; my extreme poverty shall be a great volition. I must violate myself until I have nothing, and need everything; when I need, then I shall have, because I know that it is just to give more to whoever asks for more, my demand is my size, my emptiness is my measure. One also can violate God directly, through a love full of fury.

And He shall understand that this raging and murderous greed of ours is actually our sacred and vital rage, our attempt to violate ourselves, the attempt to eat more than we can to artificially increase our hunger—in the demand of life everything is lawful, even the artificial, and the artificial is sometimes the great sacrifice one makes in order to have the essential.

But, since we are little and therefore only need little, why should little not be enough for us? Because we suspect the pleasure. As the blind grope along, we foresee the intense pleasure of living.

And if we foresee it, it's also because we feel uneasily used by God, we feel uneasily that we are being used with an intense and uninterrupted pleasure—moreover our salvation for now has been that of at least being used, we are not useless, we are intensely taken advantage of by God; body and soul and life are for just that: for the interchange and ecstasy of someone. Uneasy, we feel that we are being used every instant—but that awakens within us the uneasy desire to use as well.

And He not only allows us, but He needs to be used, being used is a way of being understood. (In all religions God demands to be loved.) In order for us to have, all we are missing is to need. Needing is always the supreme moment. As the most daring joy between a man and a woman comes when the greatness of needing is such that we feel in agony and fright: without you I could not live. The revelation of love is a revelation of neediness—blessed be the poor in spirit for theirs is the lacerating kingdom of life.

If I abandon hope, I am celebrating my neediness, and that is the greatest weight of living. And, because I owned up to my lacking, then life is at hand. Many were they who abandoned all they had, and went in search of the greater hunger.

Ah, I lost my shyness: God already is. We were already announced, and it was my own erring life that announced me to the right one. Blessedness is the continuous pleasure of the thing, the process of the thing is made of pleasure and contact with whatever is gradually more and more needed. My whole fraudulent struggle came from my not wanting to own up to the promise that is fulfilled: I did not want reality.

Since being real is owning up to the promise itself: owning up to one's own innocence and retaking the taste of which one was never aware: the taste of the living.

THE TASTE OF THE LIVING.

Which is an almost null taste. And that because things are very delicate. Ah, the attempts to taste the host.

The thing is so delicate that I am astonished it manages to be visible. And there are things even so much more delicate that they are not visible. But all of them have a delicateness equivalent to what it means for our body to have a face: the sensitization of the body that is a human face. The thing has a sensitization of itself like a face.

Ah, and I who did not know how to consubstantiate my "soul." It is not immaterial, it is of the most delicate material of thing. It is thing, I just cannot manage to consubstantiate it in visible thickness.

Ah, my love, things are very delicate. We tread upon them with a too-human hoof, with too many feelings. Only the delicateness of innocence or only the delicateness of the initiates can taste its almost null taste. Before I needed seasoning for everything, and that was how I leapt over the thing and experienced the taste of the seasoning.

I could not experience the taste of the potato, since the potato is almost the matter of the earth; the potato is so delicate that—from my incapacity to live on the level of delicateness of the merely earthy taste of the potato—I put my human hoof atop it and broke its living-thing delicateness. Because the living matter is very innocent.

And my own innocence? It hurts me. Because I also know that, on a solely human level, innocence is having the cruelty that the roach has with itself as it is slowly dying without pain; to go beyond pain is the worst cruelty. And I am afraid of that, I who am extremely moral. But now I know that I must have a much greater courage: that of having another morality, so exempt that I myself do not understand it and that scares me.

—Ah, I remembered you, who are the oldest thing in my memory. I see you once again fastening the electrical wires to fix the light socket, mindful of the positive and negative poles, and treating things with delicateness.

I didn't know I learned so much from you. What did I learn from you? I learned how to look at a person intertwining electrical wires. I learned to see you once fixing a broken chair. Your physical energy was your most delicate energy.

—You were the oldest person I ever met. You were the monotony of my eternal love, and I didn't know it. I had for you the tedium I feel on holidays. What was it? it was like water flowing in a stone fountain, and the years demarcated on the smoothness of the stone, the moss parted by the thread of running water, and the cloud overhead, and the beloved man resting, and love halted, it was a holiday, and the silence in the mosquitoes' flight. And the available present. And my slowly bored freedom, the abundance, the abundance of the body that asks not and needs not.

I did not know how to see that that was delicate love. And it seemed like tedium to me. It really was tedium. It was a search for someone to play with, the desire to deepen the air, to enter into deeper contact with the air, the air that cannot be deepened, that was destined to stay right there suspended.

I don't know, I remember it was a holiday. Ah, how I wanted pain then: it would distract me from that great divine void that I had with you. I, the goddess resting; you, upon Olympus. The great yawn of happiness? Distance following distance, and another distance and another—the abundance of space that the holiday has. That unfolding of calm energy, which I did not even understand. That already thirstless kiss upon the distracted forehead of the beloved man resting, the pensive kiss upon the already beloved man. It was a national holiday. Flags raised.

But night falling. And I could not stand the slow transformation of something that was slowly transforming into the same something, only increased by one more identical drop of time. I remember that I told you:

—I'm a little sick to my stomach, I said breathing with a certain satiety. What should we do tonight?

—Nothing, you responded so much wiser than I, nothing, it's a holiday, said the man who was delicate with things and with time.

The profound tedium—like a great love—united us. And the next morning, very early in the morning, the world was offering itself to me. The wings of things were open, it was going to be hot in the afternoon, you could already feel it in the fresh sweat of those things that had passed the listless night, as in a hospital where the patients still awaken alive.

But all that was too refined for my human hoof. And I, I wanted beauty.

But now I have a morality that relinquishes beauty. I shall have to bid farewell with longing to beauty. Beauty was a soft enticement for me, it was the way that I, weak and respectful, adorned the thing in order to tolerate its nucleus.

But now my world is of the thing that I once called ugly or monotonous—and that no longer is ugly or monotonous to me. I went through gnawing the earth and through eating the ground, and I went through having an orgy in that, and feeling with moral horror that the earth gnawed by me also felt pleasure. My orgy really came from my puritanism: pleasure offended me, and from that offense I was making greater pleasure. Yet this world of mine now, I once would have called it violent.

Because the absence of the taste of water is violent, the absence of color in a piece of glass is violent. A violence that is all the more violent because it is neutral.

My world today is raw, it is a world of a great vital difficulty. Because, more than a star, today I want the thick and black root of the stars, I want the source that always seems dirty, and is dirty, and that is always incomprehensible.

It is with pain that I bid farewell even to the beauty of a child—I want the adult who is more primitive and ugly and drier and more difficult, and who became a child-seed that cannot be broken between the teeth.

Ah, and I also want to see if I can relinquish the horse drinking water, which is so pretty. Neither do I want my feeling because it prettifies; and could I relinquish the sky moving in clouds? and the flower? I don't want pretty love. I don't want dusk, I don't want the well-made face, I don't want the expressive. I want the inexpressive. I want the inhuman inside the person; no, it isn't dangerous, since people are human anyway, you don't have to fight for that: wanting to be human sounds too pretty to me.

I want the material of things. Humanity is drenched with humanization, as if that were necessary; and that false humanization trips up man and trips up his humanity. A thing exists that is fuller, deafer, deeper, less good, less bad, less pretty. Yet that thing too runs the risk, in our coarse hands, of becoming transformed into "purity," our hands that are coarse and full of words.

OUR HANDS THAT ARE COARSE AND FULL OF WORDS.

—Bear with my telling you that God is not pretty. And that because He is neither a result nor a conclusion, and everything we find pretty is sometimes only because it is already concluded. But what is ugly today shall be seen centuries from now as beauty, because it shall have completed one of its movements.

I no longer want the completed movement that never is really complete, and we are the ones who complete it out of desire; I no longer want to delight in the easiness of liking a thing only because, being apparently completed, it no longer scares me, and therefore is falsely mine—I, devourer that I was of beauties.

I do not want beauty, I want identity. Beauty would be an accretion, and now I shall have to dispense with it. The world does not have the intention of beauty, and that once would have shocked me: in the world no aesthetic plane exists, not even the aesthetic plane of goodness, and that once would have shocked me. The thing is much more than that. The God is greater than goodness with its beauty.

Ah, bidding farewell to all that means such great disappointment. But it is in disappointment that the promise is fulfilled, through disappointment, through pain the promise is fulfilled, and that is why one must go through hell first: until one sees that there is a much deeper manner of loving, and that manner relinquishes the accretion of beauty. God is whatever exists, and all the contradictions are within the God, and therefore do not contradict Him.

Ah, everything in me is aching as I let go of what to me was the world. Letting go is such a harsh and aggressive gesture that the person who opens her mouth to speak of letting go should be imprisoned and kept incommunicado—I myself prefer to consider that I have temporarily taken leave of my senses, rather than having the courage to think that all of this is a truth.

—Give me your hand, don't abandon me, I swear I didn't want it either: I too lived well, I was a woman of whom you could say "life and loves of G. H." I cannot put into words what the system was, but I lived inside a system. It was as if I had organized myself inside the fact of having a stomachache because, if I no longer had it, I would also lose the marvelous hope of freeing myself one day from the stomachache: my old life was necessary to me because it was exactly its badness that made me delight in imagining a hope that, without that life I led, I would not have known.

And now I am risking an entire suitable hope, in favor of a reality so much greater that I cover my eyes with my arm in order not to have to face up to a hope that is fulfilled so now—and even before I die! So before I die. I too sear myself in this discovery: that a morality exists in which beauty is of a great fearful superficiality. Now whatever is luring me and calling me is the neutral. I have no words to express, and speak therefore of the neutral. I only have that ecstasy, which also is no longer what we called ecstasy, since it is not a peak. But that ecstasy without a peak expresses the neutral of which I speak.

Ah, speaking to me and to you is being mute. Speaking to the God is the mutest that exists. Speaking to things, is mute. I know this sounds sad to you, and to me too, since I am still addicted to the condiment of the word. And that is why muteness hurts me like a dismissal.

But I know that I must dismiss myself: contact with the thing has to be a murmur, and to speak with the God I must gather disconnected syllables. My neediness came from having lost the inhuman side—I was banished from paradise when I became human. And the true prayer is the mute inhuman oratorio.

No, I don't have to rise through prayer: I must, engorged, become a vibrating nothing. What I say to God must not make sense! If it makes sense it is because I err.

Ah, don't misunderstand me: I am not taking anything from you. What I am doing is requiring of you. I know it seems I am taking away your and my humanity. But it's the opposite: what I am wanting is to live from that initial and primordial thing that was exactly what made certain things reach the point of aspiring to be human. I am wanting for me to live from the most difficult human part: for me to live from the seed of neutral love, since it was from that source that there began to rise something that later was distorting itself in sentimentations until the nucleus was suffocated by the accretion of richness and crushed in ourselves by the human hoof. I am demanding of myself a much greater love—it is a life so much greater that it does not even have beauty.

I am having that hard courage that hurts me like the flesh that transforms itself in childbirth.

But no. I still haven't told everything.

Not that what I am going to tell now is all that's missing. Much more is missing in this story of mine to myself: father and mother, for example, are missing; I have not yet had the courage to honor them; so many humiliations I went through are missing, and which I omit because only they who are not humbled are humiliated, and instead of humiliation I should speak about my lack of humility; and humility is much more than a feeling, it is reality seen with a minimum of good sense.

A lot of what I could tell is missing. But there is something that will be indispensable to say.

(I know one thing: if I reach the end of this story, I shall go, not tomorrow, but this very day, out to eat and dance at the "Top-Bambino," I furiously need to have some fun and diverge myself. Yes, I'll definitely wear my new blue dress that flatters me and gives me color, I'll call Carlos, Josefina, Antônio, I don't really remember which of the two of them I noticed wanted me or if both of them wanted me, I'll eat crevettes à la whatever, and I know because I'll eat crevettes, tonight, tonight will be my normal life resumed, the life of my common joy, for the rest of my days I'll need my light, sweet and good-humored vulgarity, I need to forget, like everyone.)

Because I haven't told everything.

BECAUSE I HAVEN'T TOLD EVERYTHING.

I haven't told how, sitting there and unmoving, I still had not stopped looking with great disgust, yes, still with disgust at the yellowed white paste atop the roach's grayness. And I knew that as long as I was disgusted, the world would elude me and I would elude me. I knew that the basic error in living was being disgusted by a roach. Being disgusted by kissing the leper was my erring the first life within me—since being disgusted contradicts me, contradicts my matter within me.

Then the one thing that I, out of pity for myself, didn't want to think, then I thought it. I could no longer hold myself back, and I thought what really was already thought.

Now, out pity for the anonymous hand I am holding in mine, out of pity for what that hand is not going to understand, I don't want to take it with me to the horror to which I went yesterday, alone.

Because what I suddenly found out is that the moment had come not only to understand that I must no longer transcend, but the instant had come to really no longer transcend. And to have now what I used to think should be for tomorrow. I'm trying to spare you, but I can't.

Because redemption had to be in the thing itself. And redemption in the thing itself would be putting into my mouth the white paste of the roach.

At the very idea, I shut my eyes with the power of someone locking her teeth, and I clenched my teeth so hard that any more and they would have broken inside my mouth. My entrails were saying no, my paste was rejecting the roach's.

I had stopped sweating, once again I had entirely dried. I tried to reason with my disgust. Why would I be disgusted by the paste coming out of the roach? had I not drunk of the white milk that is liquid maternal paste? and on drinking the thing of which my mother was made, had I not called it, namelessly, love? But reason was getting me nowhere, except with teeth clenched as though made of shivering flesh.

I couldn't.

There was only one way I could: if I gave myself a hypnotic command, and then as if I had fallen asleep and acted somnambulistically—and when I opened my eyes from sleep, I already would have "done," and it would be like a nightmare from which one wakes free because it was while sleeping that one lived through the worst.

But I knew that that was not how I should do it. I knew that I would have to eat the paste of the roach, but eat it all of me, and eat it also my own fear. Only then would I have what suddenly seemed to me would be the anti-sin: eating the paste of the roach is the anti-sin, sin would be my easy purity.

The anti-sin. But at what a price.

At the price of traversing a sensation of death.

I got up and took a step forward, with the determination not of a suicide but of a murderer of myself.

The sweat now started again, I was now sweating from head to toe, my sticky toes sliding inside my slippers, and the root of my hair was softening that viscous thing that was my new sweat, a sweat I didn't recognize and that smelled like what comes from dried-up earth after the first rains. That deep sweat was however what enlivened me, I was slowly swimming through my oldest primeval soup, the sweat was plankton and pneuma and pabulum vitae, I was being, I was me being.

No, my love, it wasn't good like what's called good. It was what's called bad. Really very, very bad. Since my root, which I was only now tasting, had the flavor of potato-tuber, mixed with the earth from which it had been torn. Yet that bad taste had a strange grace of life that I can only understand if I felt it again and can only explain by feeling it again.

I took one more step. But instead of moving forward, I suddenly threw up the milk and bread I had eaten for breakfast.

Entirely shaken by the violent vomit, which had not even been preceded by the warning of nausea, disillusioned with myself, frightened by my lack of strength to go through with the gesture that seemed to me the only one that could unite my body to my soul.

Despite myself, after throwing up, I calmed down, my forehead refreshed, and physically peaceful.

Which was worse: now I would have to eat the roach but without the help of the earlier exaltation, the exaltation that would have acted in me like a hypnosis; I had vomited the exaltation. And unexpectedly, after the revolution that is vomiting, I felt physically simple as a girl. It would have to be this way, like a girl who was unintentionally happy, that I would eat the paste of the roach.

So I stepped forward.

My joy and my shame came upon waking from the faint.

No, it hadn't been a faint. It had been more of a dizziness, since I was still standing, resting my hand on the wardrobe. A dizziness that made me lose track of moments and of time. But I knew, even before thinking, that, while I took leave of myself in the dizziness, "something had been done."

I didn't want to think but I knew. I was afraid of tasting in my mouth what I was tasting, I was afraid of running my hand across my lips and finding traces. And I was afraid of looking at the roach—which now should have less white paste upon its opaque back....

I was ashamed of having gone dizzy and unconscious in order to do something that I would never again know how I had done—since before doing it I had removed from myself all participation. I had not wanted "to know."

So that was how things were processed? "Not knowing"—so that was how the deepest things happened? some thing would always, always have to be apparently dead in order for the living to process? I'd had to not know that I was alive? Was the secret of never escaping from the greater life living like a sleepwalker?

Or was living like a sleepwalker the greatest act of trust? closing one's eyes in dizziness, and never knowing what went on.

Like a transcendence. Transcendence, which is the memory of the past or the present or the future. In me was transcendence the only way I could reach the thing? Since even eating of the roach, I had acted to transcend the very act of eating it. And now all I had was the vague memory of a horror, all I had was the idea.

Until the memory got so strong that all my body screamed inside itself.

I tensed my fingernails on the wall: I now felt the nastiness in my mouth, and then began to spit, to furiously spit that taste of no such thing, taste of a nothing that nonetheless seemed almost sweetened to me like certain flower petals, taste of myself—I was spitting out myself, without ever reaching the point of feeling that I had finally spit out my whole soul. "———because you are lukewarm, and neither hot nor cold, I will spit you out of My mouth," it was the Apocalypse according to Saint John, and the phrase that must refer to other things I no longer remembered, the phrase came to me from the depths of memory, standing for the insipid of which I had eaten—and I was spitting.

Which was difficult: because the neutral thing is extremely energetic, I was spitting and it was still I.

I only halted in my fury when I understood with surprise that I was undoing everything I had laboriously done, when I understood that I was renouncing myself. And that, alas, I was only up to my own life.

I stopped astonished, and my eyes filled with tears that only burned and did not flow. I think I did not even judge myself worthy that tears should flow, I lacked the first pity for myself, which allows crying, and in my pupils I retained in ardor the tears that were salting me and that I did not deserve to flow.

But, even without flowing, the tears were in some way companions and bathed me in some way with commiseration, so that I started lowering a consoled head. And, like someone returning from a journey, I returned to sitting quietly on the bed.

I who had thought that the best proof of the transmutation of me into myself would be putting the white paste of the roach in my mouth. And that that way I would draw near to whatever is ... divine? to whatever is real? The divine for me is whatever is real.

THE DIVINE FOR ME IS WHATEVER IS REAL.

But kissing a leper is not even goodness. It is self-reality, self-life—even if that also means the leper's salvation. But it is first of all one's own salvation. The saint's greatest benefit is to himself, which does not matter: since when he reaches his own great largeness, thousands of people are enlarged by his largeness and live from it, and he loves others as much as he loves his own terrible enlargement, he loves his enlargement with impiety for himself. Does the saint want to purify himself because he feels the need to love the neutral? to love whatever is not accretion, and to relinquish the good and the pretty. The great goodness of the saint—is that to him everything is the same. The saint sears himself until he reaches the love of the neutral. He needs that for himself.

I then understood that, in whatever fashion, living is a goodness toward others. Living is enough, and that itself ends up in the great goodness. He who lives totally is living for others, he who lives his own largeness is making an offering, even if his life takes place within the incommunicability of a cell. Living is such a great offering that thousands of people benefit from every life lived.

—Does it pain you that the goodness of the God is neutrally continuous and continuously neutral? But what I once wanted as a miracle, what I called a miracle, was really a desire for discontinuity and interruption, the desire for an anomaly: I called a miracle exactly that moment in which the true continuous miracle of the process was interrupted. But the neutral goodness of the God is still more appealable than if it were not neutral: to have it all you must do is go, to have it all you must do is ask.

And the miracle can be requested, and had, since continuity has interstices that do not discontinue it, the miracle is the note between two notes of music, it is the number between number one and number two. To have it all you have to do is need it. Faith—is knowing you can go and eat the miracle. Hunger, that is what faith is in itself—and needing is my guarantee that to me it will always be given. Needing is my guide.

No. I did not need to have had the courage to eat the paste of the roach. Since I lacked the humility of the saints: I had given to the act of eating it a meaning of "maximum." But life is divided into qualities and kinds, and the law is that the roach shall only be loved and eaten by another roach; and that a woman, in the hour of love for a man, that woman is living her own kind. I understood that I had already done the equivalent of living the paste of the roach—for the law is that I must live with the matter of a person and not of a roach.

I understood that, by placing in my mouth the paste of the roach, I was not stripping myself as the saints do, but was once again yearning for the accretion. The accretion is easier to love.

And now I am not taking your hand for myself. I am the one giving you my hand.

Now I need your hand, not so that I won't be scared, but so that you won't. I know that believing in all this will be, at first, your great solitude. But the moment will come when you will give me your hand, no longer out of solitude, but as I am doing now: out of love. Like me, you will no longer fear adding yourself to the extreme energetic sweetness of the God. Solitude is having only the human destiny.

And solitude is not needing. Not needing leaves a man very alone, all alone. Ah, needing does not isolate the person, the thing needs the thing: all you have to do is see the chick walking around to see that its destiny will be what neediness makes of it, its destiny is to join as drops of mercury join other drops of mercury, even if, like each drop of mercury, it has in itself an entirely complete and round existence .

Ah, my love, do not be afraid of neediness: it is our greater destiny. Love is so much more fatal than I had thought, love is as inherent as wanting itself, and we are guaranteed by a necessity that shall renew itself continuously. Love already is, it is always. All that is missing is the coup de grâce—which is called passion.

ALL THAT IS MISSING IS THE COUP DE GRÂCE — WHICH is called passion.

What I am feeling now is a joy. Through the living roach I am coming to understand that I too am whatever is alive. Being alive is a very high stage, it is something that I only reached now. It is such a high unstable equilibrium that I know I shall not be able to know about that equilibrium for long—the grace of passion is short.

Maybe, being man, like us, is only a special sensitization we call "having humanity." Oh, I too fear losing that sensitization. Until now I had called life my sensitivity to life. But being alive is something else.

Being alive is a coarse radiating indifference. Being alive is unattainable by the finest sensitivity. Being alive is inhuman— the deepest meditation is so empty that a smile exhales as from a matter. And even more delicate shall I be, and as a more permanent state. Am I speaking of death? am I speaking of after death? I don't know. I feel that "not human" is a great reality, and that it does not mean "unhuman," to the contrary: the not-human is the radiating center of a neutral love in Hertzian waves.

If my life is transformed into it-self, the thing I today call sensitivity will not exist—it will be called indifference. But I cannot yet grasp that way. It is as if hundreds of thousands of years from now we are finally no longer what we feel and think: we shall have something that more closely resembles a "mood" than an idea. We shall be the living matter revealing itself directly, ignorant of word, surpassing thought which is always grotesque.

And I shall not wander "from thought to thought," but from mood to mood. We shall be inhuman—as the loftiest conquest of man. Being is being beyond human. Being man does not work, being man has been a constraint. The unknown awaits us, but I feel that this unknown is a totalization and will be the true humanization for which we longed. Am I speaking of death? no, of life. It is not a state of happiness, it is a state of contact.

Ah, don't think this all doesn't nauseate me, I even find it so tiresome that it makes me impatient. Because it seems like heaven, where I cannot even imagine what I would do, since I can only imagine myself thinking and feeling, two attributes of being, and I cannot imagine merely being, and relinquishing the rest. Just being—that would give me an enormous lack of things to do.

At the same time I was also a bit suspicious.

Because, just as before when I had frightened myself by entering what could end up being despair, I now suspected that I was once again transcending things....

Could I be excessively enlarging the thing precisely in order to surpass the roach and the piece of iron and the piece of glass?

I don't think so.

Since I was not even reducing hope to a simple result of constructing and counterfeiting, nor denying that something to hope for exists. Nor had I removed the promise: I was simply feeling, with an enormous effort, that the hope and the promise are fulfilled every instant. And that was terrifying, I was always afraid of being struck down by completion, I had always thought that completion is an end—and had not counted on the ever-born need.

And also because I feared, unable to bear simple glory, turning it into yet another accretion. But I know—I know—that there is an experience of glory in which life has the purest taste of the nothing, and that in glory I feel it empty. When living comes to pass, one wonders: but was that it? And the answer is: that is not only it, that is exactly it.

Except I still must be careful not to make more of it than this, or else it will no longer be it. The essence is of a pungent insipidity. I will have "to purify myself" much more in order not to even want the accretion of events. Purifying myself once meant a cruelty against what I called beauty, and against what I called "I," without knowing that "I" was an accretion of myself.

But now, through my most difficult fright—I am finally heading toward the inverse path. I head toward the destruction of what I built, I head for depersonalization.

I am avid for the world, I have strong and defined desires, tonight I'll go dance and eat, I won't wear the blue dress, but the black-and-white one. But at the same time I need nothing. I don't even need for a tree to exist. I now know of a way that relinquishes everything—and including love, nature, objects. A way that does without me. Though, as for my desires, my passions, my contact with a tree—they are still for me like a mouth eating.

Depersonalization as the dismissal of useless individuality—losing everything one can lose and, even so, being. Little by little stripping, with an effort so mindful that one does not feel the pain, stripping, like getting rid of one's own skin, one's characteristics. Everything that characterizes me is just the way that I am most easily visible to others and how I end up being superficially recognizable to myself. As there was the moment in which I saw that the roach is the roach of all roaches, so do I want to find in me the woman of all women.

Depersonalization as the great objectification of oneself. The greatest exteriorization one can reach. Whoever gets to oneself through depersonalization shall recognize the other in any disguise: the first step in relation to the other is finding inside oneself the man of all men. Every woman is the woman of all women, every man is the man of all men, and each of them could appear wherever man is judged. But only in immanence, because only a few reach the point of, in us, recognizing themselves. And then, by the simple presence of their existence, revealing ours.

Whatever we live from—and because it has no name only muteness pronounces it—it is from that that I draw closer to myself through the great largess of letting myself be. Not because I then find the name of the name and the impalpable becomes concrete—but because I designate the impalpable as impalpable, and then the breath breaks out anew as in a candle's flame.

The gradual deheroization of oneself is the true labor one works at beneath the apparent labor, life is a secret mission. So secret is the true life that not even to me, who am dying of it, can the password be entrusted, I die without knowing wherefrom. And the secret is such that, only if the mission manages to be accomplished shall I, in a flash, perceive that I was born in charge of it—every life is a secret mission.

The deheroization of myself is subterraneously undermining my building, coming to pass without my consent like an unheeded calling. Until it is finally revealed to me that the life in me does not bear my name.

And I too have no name, and that is my name. And because I depersonalize myself to the point of not having my name, I reply whenever someone says: I.

Deheroization is the great failure of a life. Not everyone manages to fail because it is so laborious, one first must climb painfully until finally reaching high enough to be able to fall—I can only reach the depersonality of muteness if I have first constructed an entire voice. My civilizations were necessary for me to rise to a point from which I could descend. It is exactly through the failure of the voice that one comes to hear for the first time one's own muteness and that of others and of things, and accepts it as the possible language. Only then is my nature accepted, accepted with its frightened torture, where pain is not something that happens to us, but what we are. And our condition is accepted as the only one possible, since it is what exists, and not another. And since living it is our passion. The human condition is the passion of Christ.

Ah, but to reach muteness, what a great effort of voice. My voice is the way I go in search of reality; reality, before my language, exists like a thought that is not thought, but inescapably I was and am compelled to need to know what the thought thinks. Reality precedes the voice that seeks it, but as the earth precedes the tree, but as the world precedes the man, but as the sea precedes the vision of the sea, life precedes love, the matter of the body precedes the body, and in turn language one day will have preceded the possession of silence.

I have to the extent I designate—and this is the splendor of having a language. But I have much more to the extent I cannot designate. Reality is the raw material, language is the way I go in search of it—and the way I do not find it. But it is from searching and not finding that what I did not know was born, and which I instantly recognize. Language is my human effort. My destiny is to search and my destiny is to return empty-handed. But—I return with the unsayable. The unsayable can only be given to me through the failure of my language. Only when the construction fails, can I obtain what it could not achieve.

And it is no use to try to take a shortcut and want to start, already knowing that the voice says little, starting straightaway with being depersonal. For the journey exists, and the journey is not simply a manner of going. We ourselves are the journey. In the matter of living, one can never arrive beforehand. The via crucis is not a detour, it is the only way, one cannot arrive except along it and with it. Persistence is our effort, giving up is the reward. One only reaches it having experienced the power of building, and, despite the taste of power, preferring to give up. Giving up must be a choice. Giving up is the most sacred choice of a life. Giving up is the true human instant. And this alone, is the very glory of my condition.

Giving up is a revelation.

GIVING UP IS A REVELATION.

I give up, and will have been the human person—it is only in the worst of my condition that that condition is taken up as my destiny. Existing demands of me the great sacrifice of not having strength, I give up, and all of a sudden the world fits inside my weak hand. I give up, and onto my human poverty opens the only joy granted me human joy. I know that, and I tremble—living strikes me so, living deprives me of sleep.

I climb high enough to be able to fall, I choose, I tremble and give up, and, finally, dedicating myself to my fall, depersonal, without a voice of my own, finally without me—then does everything I do not have become mine. I give up and the less I am the more I live, the more I lose my name the more they call me, my only secret mission is my condition, I give up and the less I know the password the more I fulfill the secret, the less I know the more the sweetness of the abyss is my destiny. And so I adore it.

With my hands quietly clasped on my lap, I was having a feeling of tender timid joy. It was an almost nothing, like when the breeze makes a blade of grass tremble. It was almost nothing, but I could make out the minuscule movement of my timidity. I don't know, but with distressed idolatry I was approaching something, and with the delicateness of one who is afraid. I was approaching the most powerful thing that had ever happened to me.

More powerful than hope, more powerful than love?

I was approaching something I think was—trust. Perhaps that is the name. Or it doesn't matter: I could also give it another.

I felt that my face in modesty was smiling. Or perhaps it wasn't, I don't know. I was trusting.

Myself? the world? the God? the roach? I don't know. Perhaps trusting is not a matter of what or whom. Perhaps I now knew that I myself would never be equal to life, but that my life was equal to life. I would never reach my root, but my root existed. Timidly I let myself be pierced by a sweetness that humbled me without restraining me.

Oh God, I was feeling baptized by the world. I had put a roach's matter into my mouth, and finally performed the tiniest act.

Not the maximum act, as I had thought before, not heroism and sainthood. But at last the tiniest act that I had always been missing. I had always been incapable of the tiniest act. And with the tiniest act, I had deheroized myself. I, who had lived from the middle of the road, had finally taken the first step along its beginning.

Finally, finally, my casing had really broken and without limit I was. Through not being, I was. To the ends of whatever I was not, I was. Whatever I am not, I am. All shall be within me, if I shall not be; for "I" is just one of the instantaneous spasms of the world. My life does not have a merely human meaning, it is much greater—so much greater that, as humanity goes, it makes no sense. Of the general organization that was greater than I, I had previously only perceived the fragments. But now, I was much less than human—and I would only fulfill my specifically human destiny if I handed myself over, as I was handing myself over, to whatever was no longer I, to whatever is already inhuman.

And handing myself over with the trust of belonging to the unknown. Since I can only pray to whatever I do not know. And I can only love the unknown evidence of things, and can only add myself to what I do not know. Only that is really handing myself over.

And such handing-over is the only surpassing that does not exclude me. I was now so much greater that I could no longer see myself. As great as a far-off landscape. I was far off. But perceptible in my furthest mountains and in my remotest rivers: the simultaneous present no longer scared me, and in the furthest extremity of me I could finally smile without even smiling. At last I was stretching beyond my sensibility.

The world independed on me—that was the trust I had reached: the world independed on me, and I am not understanding whatever it is I'm saying, never! never again shall I understand anything I say. Since how could I speak without the word lying for me? how could I speak except timidly like this: life just is for me. Life just is for me, and I don't understand what I'm saying. And so I adore it. ————————

Translator's Note

A FRIEND IN BRAZIL TOLD ME OF A YOUNG WOMAN IN Rio who'd read Clarice Lispector obsessively and was convinced—as I and legions of other Clarice devotees have been—that she and Clarice Lispector would have a life-changing connection if they met in person. She managed to get in touch with the writer, who kindly agreed to meet her. When the young woman arrived, Clarice sat and stared at her and said nothing until the woman finally fled the apartment.

To translate an author who is no longer alive is always a bit like this woman's encounter. You can ask a question but you don't get an answer. The author just stares at you and says nothing and you wonder if the best thing to do would be to get up and run out of the room, especially if the work you're translating is as mystifying as *The Passion According to G. H.*

I would have liked to ask about her curiously alternating use of "o Deus" ("the God") and "Deus" ("God")—how strange she intended that article to sound to the reader. I also would have liked to ask her about the various words that recur throughout the book like the subjects in a fugue, returning each time at a slightly different pitch. She uses the word *preso*, for example, to refer to a prisoner and then to the figures in a bas-relief on a wall and then to the narrator's feeling as she stands inside the dry, hot room of her former maid where the entire novel takes place.

I knew one of my priorities as the translator of this novel had to be recreating the fugue-like repetitions of words like *preso* throughout the novel, but in several instances using "imprisoned" made the sentence sound odd in English in a way it didn't in the original, as when she uses *preso* to describe the sensation of being pinned under a rock. I ultimately used "pinned" instead of "imprisoned" for that instance, but wish I could have asked her: was I right to go with "pinned" here, or should I have used "imprisoned" instead, as the lyrical use of repetition is so essential to what makes this novel such a hypnotizing book?

This dilemma came up with certain moments of wordplay as well, as when she says there are so many roaches that they "parece uma prece," which literally means they "seem a prayer." That literal rendering, however, fails to capture the sonic pleasure of the phrase in the Portuguese. I ultimately went with the phrase "they appear a prayer." The repetition of the *p*'s and *r*'s offered some of the inventive lyricism of the phrase in the original, although seeming and appearing are not perfect matches sensewise. As I couldn't ask Clarice when to prioritize the music and when the meaning in this book, I had to trust what I'd come to hear in my head rereading *G. H.* many times over the past decade. This was the first work of hers I encountered in college, and I was so riveted by it that I immediately read everything else she'd written. The following year, I learned Portuguese in part to learn how her voice sounded in the original.

Even after rereading this novel so often and so intently that I know a number of passages in it by memory, I still feel as if every hair on my head has caught on fire when I reach the end of it. The experience of translating G. *H*. has left me feeling bald, and not as if I lost my hair in the process so much as discovering that like G. H., like the roach, I am actually all cilia and antennae and would never have come to know this without gradually, painstakingly experiencing every word in this book. And so—as in the last line of this finest of novels —I adore it.

IDRA NOVEY